MAKING CONTACT

Tom Romita

PROLOGUE

Nine-year-old William Dobbs sits on his bed in his baseball themed pajamas, halfheartedly flipping through the latest Sports Illustrated. The crisp, clear New England morning starkly contrasts William's somber mood. The morning sun illuminates a room full of New York Yankees memorabilia, and although being a Yankee fan in a Boston suburb could leave one in a foul mood, it is not the source of young William's sadness.

On a comparatively sparse nightstand sits a solitary framed picture. The young man and woman in the picture are smiling, and the man is holding a baby boy. William closes the magazine, takes the picture in his hand and looks at it. His focus is on the father. He is wearing a white polo shirt and a New York Yankees cap.

There is a knock on the bedroom door. William doesn't look up.

"Yeah," he says.

Stephanie Dobbs enters the room. She's thirty-three, attractive, with olive skin and chestnut-colored hair and eyes. She sees William looking at the picture and smiles sympathetically as she sits on the bed, touching his sandy blond hair.

"Hey, buddy," she says.

"Hey, Mom."

"You OK?"

"Yeah. Didn't sleep too great."

Stephanie looks at William, who doesn't seem able to raise his eyes to meet hers. She feels a wave of helplessness, that of a mother whose child is hurting, and there isn't anything she can do about it.

"I know," she says, gently rubbing his back. "I'm sorry, sweetheart. We knew there would never really be a good time to tell you, but we also knew the time would come. When you were little you wouldn't have understood, and now that you're getting big, we didn't want to keep the truth from you for too long. Does that make sense?"

"I know. I understand."

Understanding doesn't make it hurt any less. William looks at the picture again, places it on his lap and sits still, staring at the sunlight glinting off dust floating around the room. He bursts into tears and hugs his mother.

"Why would he? Why would he do that to me?" William says.

"It's OK. It's OK," his mother says, holding her son close. "We don't know, Will. We may never know. It may have just not been possible for him to raise a baby boy by himself. He left you in a safe place because he loved you and wanted the best for you. Just like me and your dad."

William calms as his mother holds him and kisses his head.

"I mean, I was always a little sad that my real mom and dad died in, you know… the accident." William glances at an old scar on his left forearm. "But I don't remember them really. Now that I know my real dad didn't die, and is maybe still alive, now it's like I'm sad all over again."

"I know, Will. I know how hard it is. Just know your father and I love you as if you were our own. We will do everything we can to make this hurt less."

William breathes deeply. He says with a newfound resolve, "I want my father."

As Stephanie is holding William, trying to find the words to comfort her son, she's taken aback by his sudden fortitude. The bedroom door opens. Andrew Dobbs, the boy's father, peers in. He's a kind-faced, somewhat typical soccer dad, who happens to have a baseball-obsessed son. He's wearing a suit and adjusting the tie that completes his corporate commuter uniform.

"Hey," he asks. "How are we?"

"My real father," says William. Andrew stops adjusting his tie as Stephanie looks up at him, silently asking for patience.

"William," Stephanie says, "We told you because we thought you were old enough."

"I know," William says. "I am. I'm sorry. I love you and dad. I just want to meet him. That's all." The tears had almost stopped, but William wipes one more from his cheek. "It just hurts."

Andrew resumes his tie knotting. "That is something we can talk about in the future. As we told you, he left no contact information. We know his name was… or is, Carlton Rossi. He just left you and that picture in the bassinet. I don't know that it's possible to find him."

William sighs, picks up the framed picture, and looks at it. He has had this photo all his life but now he can't get himself to stop looking at it. His young eyes are blurred from tears but clear in their conviction, as an idea comes to him.

"I think it is," says William. "And I know how."

Stephanie holds William tightly and kisses his head to comfort him, but his sadness has evolved into dogged determination, as he focuses on the man in the picture. The man in the Yankees baseball hat.

CHAPTER 1

Camera flashes ignite the room as 23-year-old William "Will" Dobbs, wearing a suit and tie and Yankees hat, holds up a #17 New York Yankees jersey. His smile is almost as bright as the flashes. Will shakes hands with team managers and Yankee brass, accepting congratulations from all. A reporter blurts out a question.

"Will! You just signed the second biggest rookie contract in Yankee history. You up to the challenge?"

Will smiles confidently. "You know, the great thing about playing in New York is that you always know exactly how you're doing. If I'm not earning my keep, the fans will let me know."

The reporters chuckle approvingly at the young third baseman's disarming confidence.

"I'm looking forward to hearing a lot more cheers than jeers," Will adds, as another reporter shouts out a question.

"Hey, Will, you've said this is a dream come true. How does a kid from Boston grow up dreaming of becoming a New York Yankee?"

Will squints through the flashes, and soon finds the source of the question. He takes a moment, and answers.

"Let's just say I'm doing it for my Dad," he says. "See you on Opening Day."

Will is whisked off by elated Yankee coaches and PR handlers as reporters futilely attempt to ask follow-up questions of the new starting third baseman for the New York Yankees.

Kerry is busy unpacking boxes in the foyer of an upscale but understated Victorian house in suburban New York, that has clearly only been recently inhabited. She is twenty-five, blonde, freckled, with blue eyes and a small nose that people often mistake for a skilled surgeon's creation.

Attractive women are often described as sultry, exotic, mysterious, or striking; Kerry was none of these. Her beauty was like a welcoming summer ocean breeze on a hot day. A mix of adorable and angelic, you could almost hear birds chirping whenever she entered a room. Her model-next-door face is currently crinkled, as she contemplates the ideal placement of a blue glass vase on a table in the foyer. It would bring out the blue in the curtains she has planned for the living room, she thinks. But is that too much blue? Is blue even a good living room color? Her head is full of plans and color schemes for all the rooms. Rooms she didn't have to think about when she lived in the two-bedroom apartment in Brighton. The "BC" apartment, "Before Contract." She smiles. There is a lot to think about, to do, but she is happy. Will emerges from the hallway with a large duffel bag over his shoulder.

"Hey, beautiful," he says. "Don't get buried under these boxes."

"Will," she says. "You leaving already?"

"Soon. Don't want to be late for the first day at the office." He looks at the wall to wall boxes. "Seriously, we have plenty of time to unpack. I'll ask the guys for some moving companies. Or decorating. Or unpacking. Whatever it is we need, I'll get it."

"Hey," Kerry says, taking Will's hands in hers. "Don't worry about the house. I've got it. You go do what you do best so we can pay for it." She smiles irresistibly.

"Come here," he says.

The mutual attraction between Will and Kerry hasn't waned an iota since the day they struck up a beer-fueled conversation at a Boston College fraternity party three and a half years ago. He told her he was a baseball player and she immediately started making football references. It took several exchanges on option routes and zone defenses before Will realized she wasn't drunk or daffy, but messing with him. At first, she had been hesitant to date a ball player, especially a young hot shot like Will. She had envisioned herself ending up with a banker or lawyer type. But after four years of college boys destined for those professional persuasions, she'd decided to open her options, and her heart, a bit more. She didn't necessarily mind the talk of work and money, but she didn't want to spend her life with someone for whom these were the end all and be all. She wanted someone with passion. Not in the sexual sense necessarily, although this was never a bad thing to have in a partner. She wanted someone who loved life, did what he did best, and loved doing it. She wanted someone she felt passion for, too. She found that in Will, and the promise of a lucrative career and the chiseled physique he'd acquired following his passion didn't hurt either.

Will Dobbs had never had trouble meeting women. From the time he made the high school varsity baseball team his Freshman year, he was attracting girls from all over Boston's South Bay. Baseball has always been like a religion around Boston, and the tall, slender boy with blond hair and hazel eyes was evolving into one of its gods. He dated, but soon tired of the drama when the relationships ended. He didn't mean to hurt anyone, or "play the field," he just tended to find that as he got to know those he dated, the less inclined he was to want to stay with them in any permanent kind of way. He was not good at breaking things off, and the women he dated, seemed even worse at it. He was able to divide the women he'd dated into two categories: those who were insecure, who didn't value themselves as highly as they should, and those who thought far too highly of themselves. Each and every girl posed a new unwelcomed challenge, and a new unhappy ending. Eventually, he just stopped dating altogether. Not that there weren't the occasional "hook ups," but he was always careful to end anything before it truly began. Will got a reputation as a player, even though he didn't have any real intention or desire to be one.

In Kerry, he found the girl he'd dreamed of, but wasn't sure existed outside his imagination—a woman with the confidence that came with being beautiful and smart, and knowing it, but also the self-awareness that these qualities did not entitle her to royal treatment, or the right to look down on or mistreat others not as lucky or gifted as she was. Kerry was as kind as she was gorgeous. He was hooked from the first night they met.

Kerry walks over to Will, who drops his duffel bag, wraps his arms around her and kisses her. He kisses her some more. She playfully pushes him away.

"I thought you didn't want to be late," she says.

"I have something for you."

"William Dobbs. What did you do?" she asks coyly.

Will pulls out a small box, drops to one knee and asks, "Will you marry me?"

Kerry takes a moment, raises an eyebrow, and holds up her left hand with a gold band on the ring finger and waggles it at Will.

"Again?" she asks.

"Yes," he says. "I just want to do it right this time."

He opens the box. It contains another gold band, but this one comes with a three-karat diamond attached to it. Kerry gasps.

"Oh my God, Will! Why?"

"You need a ring as special and beautiful as you are. Do you like it?"

"It's beautiful Will, but jeez, how much…"

Will cuts her off with a gentle, "Shhhh." He takes her hand and puts the ring on her finger. "Did you see all those zeros in my contract?" he asks. "Those are our zeros. What else should I be spending the money on?"

Kerry looks at the ring dazzling in the morning light. She smiles and hugs Will.

"I love you," she says.

"I love you, too."

"And I love the ring, but umm…"

"But what?" Will asks, concerned.

"Well, we should probably save a little to, umm, furnish that extra guest room."

"Sure, babe, we will. Don't worry, that won't cost that much."

Kerry hesitates, trying to navigate the minefield she has just voluntarily wandered into.

"No, I mean, more like… make plans for it."

Kerry touches her stomach. Will's head tilts in confusion, before his eyes widen with comprehension.

"What?! Really?! When?!" he says.

"Yesterday. I mean, I took a test yesterday," Kerry blurts. "Then another this morning. I didn't want to tell you before the first game, but I guess I couldn't help it. Sorry."

"Sorry?" Will asks. "We're gonna have a baby?"

"Yep. I know we wanted to wait," Kerry says patting her stomach again, "but apparently someone else had other plans."

Will takes a long moment, and looks as if he's going to cry.

"We're gonna have a baby," he says. He gives Kerry a big hug. "A baby. I love you so much."

"I love you, too. And I love my ring."

She looks at her ring on her hand draped around Will's neck and notices the time on her wristwatch. "You have to go!" she says. "It's your first game!"

"I feel like I should stay," Will says.

"No! Go! You'll be late. I'm fine! I'll be in my seat before kickoff."

"Haha, funny. OK. You sure?"

"Yes. Go score a touchdown. I love you. See you there."

"We're gonna have a baby," Will says again. Saying it out loud makes him happy.

"Yes, we are."

They kiss again. Will grabs his bag and heads out.

CHAPTER 2

Will arrives at the stadium early, and has to wait ten minutes to be let into the players' parking area. He parks his new two-door Audi and wonders if he should trade it in for something with a few more doors and cubic feet. He makes his way to the legendary Yankees clubhouse. Even though the new stadium is less than a decade old, it is thick in history. Will is the first and only one there. He slowly walks around, gingerly touching some of the lockers of the Yankee stars. He reaches the one with his name on it, smiles wide-eyed, and gasps slightly at the sight of his name amongst those of his heroes. He looks at the crisply pressed pinstriped uniform hanging on the bar. He still can't quite fathom seeing his name across the back. He grasps the handle of the large wooden storage drawer and tries to open it. It's stuck. He starts pulling at it, frustrated.

"Sometimes you gotta lean on that one a little."

Will is startled at the voice coming from behind him. He turns to see a man in a Yankee blue jumpsuit, holding a broom.

"Oh, hi," Will says. He walks up to the man, who appears to be in his fifties, with a weathered face, blue eyes and light brown hair turning to silver. "William Dobbs," he says.

They shake hands.

"Didn't mean to startle you," the man says after a moment. "I'm Tony, I clean up around here. Pleasure to meet you, Mr. Dobbs. I wish you the best this season."

"Thanks," says Will. "I'm a rookie."

"I know. Me too. I read about you. I'm looking forward to watching you play."

"I hope I don't disappoint you."

"I doubt that," Tony says with a kind smile.

"Thanks," says Will.

Both men look around the room, absorbing the history, reveling in their place in it.

"Kind of amazing, isn't it?" says Tony.

"I still can't believe I'm really here. About to start at third for the New York Yankees."

"This is like a dream come true for me, too," says Tony.

Will looks at Tony. As odd as it is to hear a man proclaiming that a job mopping up after a ball team is a dream come true, Will believes him.

"It's like all of my dreams come true," Will says. "It's like there's been a big hole in my life that I'm finally going to fill." Will looks around the room wistfully. "Hopefully today."

"Me too," Tony says.

"Are you a big fan?" Will asks.

"Oh yeah. Used to play too," Tony says as he knocks on his right thigh, which gives a hollow, artificial sounding 'thunk.' "'Till I lost a wheel."

"Oh," Will says. "Sorry about that."

Tony looks at Will with woeful envy, and Will starts to wish he hadn't gotten to the stadium quite so early.

"Oh no, it's all right," Tony says. "I've done… OK."

Tony tries to force a smile, but his words don't reflect the sadness in his eyes.

"I bet you could show me a thing or two," Will says, trying to lighten the mood.

"Yeah, maybe," Tony says. "I never made it to the big dance. Life throws you curveballs, ya know. But you learn to adapt. We all do. Everything does. We adapt to life, life adapts to us. Things work out, for better or worse, but things work out." He pauses, then changes course, remembering who he is talking to, and what his job is. "Anyway, I'm glad as heck they gave me the job here. And I'll be at every home game. Unless I get myself hit by a bus."

"Now you can't let that happen," Will says.

"Ha. Why zat?"

"'Cuz I'll never get into my goddamn locker."

Tony smiles wide, walks up to the stuck drawer, leans into it and then pulls. The door opens.

"Ha! Thanks," says Will.

"Ramirez apparently didn't take too well to getting cut. Took it out on his… well, your locker. I've told them to get a new one installed. Until then, push. Up and in."

Will smiles. "High and tight," he says.

Tony smiles back. "Chin music. 'Zactly. Good luck out there today, Mr. Dobbs."

"Will. Please," Will says. "Mr. Dobbs is my father."

CHAPTER 3

It's a sunny June Saturday in the Bronx, and a capacity crowd has filled Yankee stadium to watch their team take on the Baltimore Orioles. The Yankees and Orioles are in first and second place respectively in this early season division rivalry. It's the bottom of the ninth inning. The score is 1-0. There are two outs and two men are on base.

A chorus of boos rises from the crowd. Will Dobbs heads toward home plate, bat in hand. The spark that once danced in Will's eyes after signing with the Yankees has vanished. His eyes are now confused, almost suspicious. Will is frustrated and a bit angry. He looks into the inhospitable crowd, replete with stock market millionaires, soccer moms and dads and their kids. He sees some of them holding signs saying "KILL WILL," and "DOBBS ROBS." He looks toward the player's VIP boxes and catches a glimpse of Kerry, whose discomfort is not solely due to her ever-growing pregnant body. He quickly looks away. Will's parents, Stephanie and Andrew have made the trip from Boston and are sitting with Kerry, trying to be supportive. Tony the janitor is watching the game from a spot he's discovered behind an outfield wall.

In the press booth, announcer Lester Lowe and color commentator Archie Talbot are calling the game.

"Well, it's Will Dobbs coming to bat, the promising young infielder who has been, well, there's no kind way to put it, Arch," Lester says into the microphone. "He's been a disappointment so far in his short career."

Former Angel catcher Archie chimes in, "The game is in his hands Les, and yeah, it's clear that the fans, and I'm sure the Yankees themselves, are wishing it was in someone else's."

"It's too bad, he's a scrappy kid, a likeable kid," says Lester. "The Bomber from Beantown. But you're right, he's just not producing at the plate. Not at major league level. His fielding is decent, and he's got good speed, but he's batting .211 with one homer, almost mid-way through the season. What happened to this kid, Archie? I had him in the running for rookie of the year back in April."

"You know, Les, sometimes players shine in college and the minors, and then they get to the big leagues and for whatever reason, they can't hack it," says Archie. "These are the guys no one remembers, they just sorta disappear," he says, then adds solemnly, "I'm afraid we might be seeing poor Will Dobbs becoming invisible, right before our eyes."

"Well, let's see what he does here, Les. A hit could bring the Yanks a win and a winning record going into the All-Star break, and give these fans a reason to believe in the young Bomber from Beantown. Here we go."

Archie, Lester and the other fifty thousand fans settle in to watch Will take his place in the batter's box.

Will is finding it nearly impossible to focus. His mind keeps drifting to 'What if?' 'What if I don't improve?' 'What if I get cut?' 'What if this is the end?' Kerry, the baby, his father…

"Strike!" the umpire bellows from behind the plate as the boos rise from the angry throng. Will is startled by the volume.

"Big crowd today, eh Dobbs?" the catcher says, snidely.

"Shut it, Cochrane," the ump says sternly. "Play ball!"

How did this happen? Will wonders. How did he become hated? He'd never been hated before. He didn't know what to do with it. Now here he was at twenty-three, competing at the highest level of his sport, his life's passion, and fifty thousand people are presently expressing their hatred of him, in unison. He didn't know how to snap out of a slump, because he'd never been in one. He didn't know if he could. He was the star of his Little League team, so much so that the dads had to have a secret meeting with him telling him to stop hitting so many home runs, so the other boys wouldn't get discouraged. He went to B.C. on a full baseball scholarship and was drafted by the Yankees right after he graduated. He'd finally gotten to where he needed to be make all his dreams come true.

But now, three months into the season, his father had not magically appeared. Will had been driven to greatness by the hope that his proud father would find his famous son, but now that it seemed it was not to be, his drive, and his abilities on the field have drastically waned. It consumed his thoughts. Why had he not appeared? Where was he? Why had he failed? At finding his father, and now at baseball.

"Strike two!"

The boos increase in intensity. What if this wasn't a slump? What if this is it? What if he just wasn't good enough? That can't happen, Will thinks. It can't. He couldn't let that happen. He'd worked his whole life to get here, for reasons few knew, reasons bigger than fame and fortune. Bigger than baseball. He couldn't fail. Where are you…

"Ball!"

Will quickly scans the roiling crowd. As he does, he spots a man, standing out from the rest, just behind the visitors' dugout. He looks to be around fifty, and he's wearing a white shirt and a Yankees hat. He's staring at Will. Will steps out of the batter's box. Will's eyes meet the man's. The boos rise in intensity. After a few seconds, the man joins in the booing, his yells aimed directly at Will and are even louder and more vitriolic than the crowd around him.

Will looks away. He takes a deep breath and shakes his head. Of all the emotions he has felt since becoming a Yankee, he's finding it harder and harder to fight off this new one seeping into his consciousness—anger. He kicks the dirt under his feet, steps back into the box, and looks at the pitcher with a newfound focus. He knows what he has to do. The boos fade from his consciousness. He is where he needs to be. He feels like he hasn't felt in the box in months. He is ready. He digs in, laser focused on one thing—making contact. The pitcher sets, and delivers.

It must have gotten away from him. A ninety-five-mile-per-hour fastball is heading straight at Will. Will's eyes widen as he sees the ball growing larger and larger, approaching at a terrifying speed. He dives back to avoid contact, but not in time. The ball hits him squarely in the temple, sending his helmet flying as he collapses in a heap on the ground. A collective gasp echoes eerily through the stadium. The pitcher cringes.

"Oh God, no," Kerry cries, hand over her mouth.

"Get up. Get up, son!" says Andrew. Stephanie begins shaking and looking around for help.

"Will!" she cries.

"Get up, baby," Kerry says. "Just get up."

Will does not get up. He lays motionless, as medical staff from both dugouts rush onto the field. A trickle of blood collects in a small puddle in the dirt where Will's head lies. Players from both teams stand in silent unity, watching for a sign of life from their fallen brother. The crowd hums with an uneasy anticipatory drone that is only heard in these kinds of situations. Tony turns away, and walks slowly toward the clubhouse.

The announcers Archie and Lester are doing their best to reassure the millions of viewers as they watch an unconscious William Dobbs carried off the field on a stretcher. But they aren't equipped to be a part of this type of story, or the possible end to one.

"It's a game. He's just a kid," Archie says. With nothing else, he turns off his mic.

"Let's take a commercial break," Lester says. "We'll be back, and we will of course update you with any news on young Yankee, Will Dobbs."

CHAPTER 4

Kerry sits in neurosurgeon Dr. Bradford Emerson's office. She's unsuccessfully trying to make herself comfortable in a plush leather office chair. The doctor is at his desk. Diplomas and awards clutter the wall behind him. His office is well appointed, but messy, like the workspace of someone who has worked hard for all he has achieved, and continues to do so.

"Mrs. Dobbs," he says to Kerry. "We're going to do everything we can to get him back to you."

Kerry tries to be strong. She's had only brief interactions with medical staff in the four days since the accident. This is the first time she's heard a doctor refer to her husband as "not with us." Alive. But not here. The tears come.

"I'm sorry," she says as she pulls one of the ever-present tissues from her bag.

"That's all right," Dr. Emerson says. "I'm going to go over everything with you, answer any questions, and share everything I know with you. We are in no rush."

"Thank you," Kerry says, wiping her eyes. "What's going to happen to him? Do you know?"

"Not exactly. We have made great advances in brain injury and coma recovery recently, but how these things play out is still a bit of a medical mystery."

"I understand," Kerry says, and girds herself to ask the most difficult question she has ever asked anyone. "Will he wake up?"

The doctor thinks for a moment, even though he knows the answer to the question he has been asked hundreds of times before. "He could wake up tomorrow," he says. "Or he might not."

"Ever?" Kerry asks.

"Ever."

Kerry struggles to keep listening.

"OK," she says, "And if he does wake up, will he be, you know, normal? Like before?"

"This is also difficult to predict," says Dr. Emerson. "The brain, like any body part, heals and scars, but unfortunately a scar on the brain is different than on say, your knee. The scar on your knee is a permanent, visible, physical injury; on the brain, it's a mental one. When the brain is injured, the mind stops working properly. It's not like a broken arm or leg, where you just make the body part physically capable of functioning again. With brain injury comes damage to thinking, sensing, remembering, feeling, behaving. It's very complicated, inexact, and depends on the severity and location of the injury. Some people have actually emerged from comas with improved mental skills. There was an Australian man who woke up from one, able to speak fluent Mandarin Chinese, though he never had before."

"Really?"

"I'm not saying Will is going to wake up a concert pianist or architect. Just making the point, brain injuries are—well, this isn't the medical term—but, they're weird."

Kerry thinks about this for a moment. "OK. What would be the worst-case scenario? I mean, if he does wake up?"

"Well," says the doctor. "He could have severe mental and physical impairment. Be confined to a wheelchair. Not able to speak or function without assistance."

Kerry's eyes begin to well. She stifles a sob.

"Well, hold on now, you asked me for the worst case," the doctor says. "There's a best, too."

"What's that?"

The doctor looks at Kerry and thinks for a moment. "When are you due?" he asks.

Kerry touches her stomach and smiles through her sadness. "January," she says.

"Best case," says Dr. Emerson, "is that William is there to take you and your baby home from the hospital."

Kerry looks up, her face hopeful. "A full recovery?" she asks.

"It is possible," Dr. Emerson says.

"What are the chances?" asks Kerry. "Of a full recovery, I mean."

Dr. Emerson adjusts some papers on his desk and folds his hands in front of him. "Let's not think in those terms, the chances," he says, "I've found that kind of thinking to be… unproductive. Right now, let's focus on giving Will the best care available, and hope for the best."

Kerry reluctantly accepts this dismissal from the doctor, although she understands its real meaning. The chances are not good.

"Is he in pain?" she asks.

"No," says Dr. Emerson. "In coma patients, the brain basically shuts off due to the trauma that has occurred in the individual. He's not feeling anything."

This is not as comforting as Kerry would have hoped. Her husband can't feel anything. Everything they might feel in the future, they won't. Everything they felt together in the past, gone. Is he even alive?

"Does he dream? I'm sorry," Kerry says. "That's a silly question."

Dr. Emerson looks at her and gives her a soothing smile.

"There have been cases in which a patient awakens and reports dreamlike visions they have had while in the coma," he says. "There is evidence that this may occur as the patient is close to waking up."

"Thank you, Doctor," Kerry says. "Thank you for taking care of Will."

"It's my job. And my pleasure. You take care of yourself and your baby. We're doing everything that can possibly be done for Will."

Against doctors' advice, Kerry spends most of the next eight weeks in Will's hospital room. The medical team promise they'll call the moment anything changes, but she can't bear the thought of leaving Will alone, or worse, not being there, if, and when he wakes up. As Will's condition remains dire, his son is growing inside Kerry's womb. She hopes that the all-encompassing sadness she is feeling won't have a negative effect on her baby. She reads books on infant care and cries every time there is a mention of a husband or partner. She tries to force an artificial happiness upon herself for her child's sake, but can't find any lasting peace, seeing the man she loves, the father of her unborn child, lying on a hospital bed in exactly the same unconscious form every day, medical lines and tubes entering and leaving multiple ports in his poor shattered body. A small scar visible at the hairline above his left ear the only direct evidence of the violence that made him this way.

Two pictures sit on the hospital bedside table—a wedding picture of Will and Kerry, and the picture of Will as a baby in his parents' arms.

The nurses have set up a reclining chair for Kerry next to Will's bed. She sleeps in it, but not well. She doesn't sleep well at home either. She is too sad to sleep, her subconscious mind replaying the moment Will was struck, over and over. When she does sleep, her dreams are terrifying, often involving conjured visions of herself giving birth to her child, alone in a barren wasteland. These nightmares disrupt the rare restful moments she has.

Today, however, Kerry is resting peacefully in the hospital room, dreaming of Will, awake and healthy, teaching their son how to hit a baseball in their back yard as she watches them happily from the back porch.

Kerry doesn't know that just a few feet away from her, Will is dreaming as well. He dreams he is sitting in a car seat in the back of a late 80s sedan, twenty-two years ago. His father, the man in the picture, is at the wheel; his mother is in the front passenger seat. They are driving along a flat, desolate country road. His mother looks back and smiles at him.

"Hey booboo," she says. "How's my big boy?"

Will can't speak, as much as he wants to. He knows what he wants to say, but he can't make his body function in order to form the words. He tries, but nothing comes out.

He begins to cry. His mother touches his leg which calms him down.

In the hospital room, Kerry stirs, roused by a beeping sound from one of the array of monitors, this one indicating an elevation in Will's heart rate. She touches his leg to calm him down.

"It's OK, Will," she says quietly.

"It's OK, Will," Will's mother says in the dream from the front seat of the car. "Almost there." She turns to her husband. "How much further?"

"We're close," he says. "Just past this intersection."

"How are you feeling?" she asks.

"Good. Ready. I feel good about this one."

"That's what you said about the last two," she answers.

"Hannah, I know, believe me, I know. It's different. I haven't had a drink in over a month now. I'm done. This is the one," he says confidently. "The Reading Phillies need a left fielder badly. They just lost theirs to the big leagues. It's gonna happen this time. I feel it."

Will's mother tries to be supportive, but feels it's her duty to make sure her husband's dreams and demons don't endanger her child's well-being.

"OK, I just… Well, we sorta need it to happen," she says.

"I know Hannah, I know. I'm going to take care of you and Will."

"OK, I know, but to—"

His mother's thought, as well as Will's dream, are interrupted by a violent impact to the passenger side of the sedan that explodes with a sickening crunch of metal and shattering glass, as a pick-up truck barrels into the sedan at fifty miles per hour.

In the hospital room, Will's eyes jolt open. Kerry senses something and sits up in her chair. She sees Will's eyes open.

"Oh my God! Will!" she cries. "Doctor! Doctor! Hurry! He's awake! Will's awake!"

Inside the mangled sedan, Will's father regains consciousness. His wife has been thrown from the vehicle. It is clear that she is beyond help, as is the driver of the pick-up.

The sedan bursts into flames. He tries to free himself from the burning wreckage, but his right leg has been shattered. His pain is replaced by panic, when he hears the desperate cries of a baby from the back seat of the car.

After months of investigation, none of the detectives, doctors, forensic experts, or Will's father himself could figure out how he was able to free himself and his one-year-old son from the burning car, and drag them to safety, thirty yards away, with only one functioning leg.

Kerry gets up and touches Will's face. He is awake but wide-eyed and panicky.

"It's OK, baby, it's OK. I love you. Doctor's coming."

A nurse enters the room and sees that Will is, in fact, awake.

"Well, good morning, Mr. Dobbs," she says. "Welcome back. Dr. Emerson is right behind me."

Will sees the nurse, but his eyes quickly leave her and dart around the room wildly. He suddenly sits up, yells and starts violently thrashing, pulling at the lines in his arms and trying to shake the oxygen mask off his face. An IV pole that was standing next to the bed crashes to the ground. Kerry gasps and steps back, frightened.

"Dr. Emerson!" the nurse yells. "Get in here, stat! And bring an orderly!" She looks at Kerry, who has instinctively put her hands over her swollen belly. "Get back!" the nurse says to her. Kerry moves to the far end of the room beyond the foot of the bed as the nurse looks at Will and moves slowly toward him. "Calm down, Mr. Dobbs. You are in a hospital, you are in good hands. The doctor will be right—"

Will lunges at the nurse, causing her to jump back, and Kerry to scream. Will's momentum carries him forward, and not having control over most of his body, he begins to fall off the bed. Just then, Dr. Emerson and an orderly arrive. They are able to grab Will and with great effort lay him back down safely. Will violently struggles. Another orderly enters, a large one, and the two are able to hold Will down to an extent, allowing Dr. Emerson to step back and try to assess the situation.

"Get off me!" Will yells, his voice hoarse and savage. "Let me go!"

Kerry is shaking. "What's wrong?!" she asks. "What's going on?"

Dr. Emerson folds his hands behind his back and speaks to Kerry in a low voice, "It's OK, this is normal. Patients emerging from comas are in a state of shock. Their brains are not used to the stimuli of the real world. They can be confused and violent. He might not know where he is or who you or any of us are. He will. It will pass."

"Get. The Hell! Off ME!!" Will yells, and Kerry looks to Dr. Emerson.

"Hopefully soon," he says. He addresses Will. "OK, Mr. Dobbs. You have been through a lot, but you are recovering. Try to calm down, we'll explain everything. You are OK. You are in good hands. We are very happy to see you."

The doctor's words seem to have the reverse of their intended effect on Will. He becomes more agitated and thrashes against the grip of the orderlies.

"URRRRGGHHH! Get off of me! I want to get out of here!!"

"Calm down! Calm. DOWN!" shouts an orderly.

"Will! Will, baby. Look! Will!" shouts Kerry. "It's me!"

Will looks at Kerry wild-eyed. He doesn't recognize her. He struggles harder.

"Let me go!! Arrrrgghh!!"

"Will," says Dr. Emerson. "That's your wife, Kerry. Do you remember her?"

"I don't have a wife!" Will shouts. "Who are you?! What did you do to me?! Where's my father?!"

The orderlies are having no success controlling or calming Will. Dr. Emerson says to the nurse, "Prepare eight milligrams of Haloperidol."

The nurse rushes out of the room.

"What's that?" Kerry asks.

"Haldol. It will sedate him." says Dr. Emerson.

Kerry looks at Will, and the thought of her husband, finally awake, about to be put under sedation again is not something she wants to consider.

"UNNNGGHHH!!! Let go! LET GO!" Will screams and flails. His elbow strikes the larger orderly in the jaw, causing him to stumble back, leaving one orderly to try to hold Will down.

"Joanne!" Dr. Emerson yells out the door.

Kerry has an idea. She touches her coat, then her bag, then looks at the framed pictures on the bedside table. She quickly moves toward them.

"Kerry, don't!" Dr. Emerson says as Kerry moves within arms' length of Will. The second orderly gets up just in time to help keep Will at bay.

Kerry ignores the doctor, first touches the wedding picture, then grabs other one, and thrusts it into Will's view. Will's wild eyes lock on the picture. He is breathing heavily, but begins to calm. He blinks. Recognition and calmness wash over him, as he slowly returns to his former self. Groggy but no longer wild-eyed, Will looks around the room. He sees Kerry.

"Kerry," he says.

Kerry starts to cry.

Dr. Emerson nods calmly to the orderlies who loosen their grip, and step back cautiously.

"Hi, baby," Kerry says. "Hi, my love. Welcome back."

The nurse rushes into the room with a syringe and another orderly. They see Will sitting calmly.

"We're OK now. Thank you," Dr. Emerson says. "Are you OK?" He asks the orderly who took an elbow to the jaw.

"I got clocked by Will Dobbs. I'm all good, all good," he says, smiling, rubbing his jaw.

"Sorry about that," Will says, looking around. "What happened to me? Why am I here? Kerry, you look tired. And big. Are you OK? Is the baby OK?"

Kerry holds his hand with one of hers and wipes away a tear with the other. "We're fine, Will," she says. "I could not be any better."

"William, I'm Dr. Emerson. My team and I have been working with you since you went into coma eight weeks ago. Welcome back."

"A coma?" Will asks.

"Try to relax," says Dr. Emerson. "We will tell you everything. Don't try to move yet, just relax. Just going to take a quick look, OK?"

Will nods and Dr. Emerson pulls a pen light from his breast pocket and shines it in Will's eyes.

"Is he OK?" asks Kerry.

"He's been through a lot," the doctor answers. "Time will tell. Follow my finger with your eyes Will… good."

"Did I get hit by a pitch?" Will asks, rubbing his head.

"Yes," the doctor says. "Keep following…"

"But this," Kerry says, "I mean, he's awake, this is good, right?"

Dr. Emerson squeezes Will's toe.

"Feel that?" he asks.

"Yes," Will answers. "Did we win?"

"Not sure, I'm a Mets fan." Will looks at him. "I'm kidding," the doctor says, smiling. He squeezes one on the other toe. "That too?" he asks.

"Yep," Will says.

Dr. Emerson steps away from the bed and says to Kerry, "Yes. Absolutely. Today is a good day."

Kerry is crying again, but now it's tears of joy and relief. "Can I hug him?" she asks.

"Absolutely," he says.

Kerry bursts into tears and hugs and kisses Will. Will closes his eyes in response. A tear rolls down his cheek.

CHAPTER 5

The Yankee brass arrange a televised press conference from the hospital to announce the good news. Yankee Owner Ted Beasley, Manager Phil Taylor, and PR Chief Ken Albrecht are sitting at a large table at one end of a conference room, filled with mostly local reporters, and a few TV cameras. Will and Kerry are also at the table. Everyone has a microphone in front of them. Kerry has to sit back from the table to avoid bumping it with her belly.

Most kids grow up with dreams of being on a baseball team. Ted Beasley dreamed of owning a baseball team. He's a large man who played football at LSU and traded his helmet for his stockbroker's license after graduation. He ran his investing empire with the same tenacity he employed on the gridiron, eventually amassing a fortune large enough to buy himself what he'd always wanted.

While he's genuinely glad to see Will's recovery, Ted can't forget that before Will got beaned, he was playing horribly, and management was in the midst of figuring out what to do with him. If he is ever able to play again, cutting a kid who defied death and has a child to feed would be a PR nightmare. Not to mention, he's still under contract, so if the medical staff deems him able to play, he still gets paid, not matter how much he stinks. Ted has dealt with a lot of curveballs and crises in his time, but never one quite as financially and emotionally prickly as this one. He would figure it out when the time came, but that time was not today.

"Well, I would just like to say, on behalf of the New York Yankees, how happy we are to have William back, so to speak," Ted says to the crowd. "Even in his brief time with the team before he got injured, he became part of the family, so we are thrilled that he's on the mend. Will, we wish you a speedy and full recovery, and when the time comes, we'll talk business."

Vice President of Public Relations Ken Albrecht is a wiry, Ivy League type, with an exclusively Brooks Brothers wardrobe and tortoiseshell glasses. He crops his naturally curly brown hair short, so as not to disrupt the neat, simple look. He played Little League ball, but once he learned statistics in Middle School, he was more excited crunching the numbers behind baseball than playing the game itself. He secured an internship with the Yankees right out of Fordham, and never left.

"Yes," Ken says, "the entire organization wishes you the best and wants you to focus on your recovery so we can see you back on the field." Ken is also personally thrilled at Will's recovery, but knows all too well of the PR tsunami headed his way, and who gets washed out to sea if the Yankees don't come out of this all looking like heroes.

Manager Phil Taylor, a tall, solid man of fifty with a full head of prematurely white hair speaks next, in a commanding voice and hint of an accent acquired by being raised nowhere near an ocean. He would much rather be in the dugout commanding the action on the diamond than in a hospital conference room full of reporters. He knows what these reporters and the fans don't—the athletes who make it this far in professional sports are literally superheroes. They do things that "normal" humans cannot, and should not, be able to do. Losing just ten percent of their abilities makes them mere mortals, no longer able to compete in the big leagues. He's glad to see the kid up and about, but has very little faith in his successful return to the game.

"Now, Will wants to say a few words," Phil says. "But guys, he needs to rest, so he's not going to take any questions. All in due time, clear?"

Murmurs of reluctant compliance from the press pool fill the room. As the grumbling settles, Will leans into the microphone. Flashes pop and reporters begin tapping on keyboards, all trying to capture the essence of the extraordinary moment. A few old-timers scribble on note pads. One of the scribblers is Stan Greenwald from the New York Post. A consummate New Yorker from a different era than many in the room, Stan hunches in his chair in khakis, a tweed coat, and beige Hush Puppies. His thick, wild, graying hair, squinty eyes and wiry eyebrows make him look like he's eternally battling a stiff wind, even indoors. Digital media is pushing old-timers like Stan, and the papers they write on, out of existence, but even after all these years, Stan still loves the hunt for the story. He knows his time is short, and he's not going to bow out quietly. He was critical of the lucrative contract Will Dobbs was offered, and even more so after he failed to deliver. This injury brought an all new wrinkle to the story, and Stan is wondering how it, and his hunt, is going to end. He, along with millions of television viewers, looks at Will in anticipation, very interested in what he has to say. With a bit of effort, Will speaks.

"Hello," Will says. "Sorry if I talk a little slow. I was pretty much a turnip last week so… cut me some slack."

The room laughs, relieved by the levity. Kerry rolls her eyes and smiles.

"I just want to say, first, thanks for all the support from the fans, and everybody at the Yankees organization. The letters and emails and everything have been amazing, they keep me going. Thanks to Dr. Emerson and his team for all they have done, and of course, to Kerry here. I couldn't stay in a coma too long knowing she was waiting for me to wake up. I love you."

Kerry blinks away a few tears, smiles and mouths "I love you too," back to Will. He continues.

"Umm… I'm feeling good, better every day. Oh, and before I forget, Dennehy, I know you didn't mean it. No hard feelings, brother, feel free to bring the chin music when I come back…"

"When will you be back, Will?" a random reporter yells.

"What the fuck did I just say, Hank?!" yells Phil Taylor.

A producer standing near the main broadcast camera winces at the F-bomb that was just dropped on live TV.

"Sorry… sorry. Sorry." Phil apologizes to everyone and no one in particular, and meekly nods and gestures for Will to continue.

"No, coach, it's OK. I'll answer," Will says. "In fact… I'll make a guarantee. I will be back playing third base for the Yankees Opening Day next season."

This bold declaration sends an excited murmur through the press pool, while Kerry and the Yankee representatives awkwardly offer very little in the way of a reaction.

Will, slightly miffed at their lack of support, continues with conviction. "There is no other option," he says. "I will be back. So right now, if you'll excuse me… I've got a lot of rehab to do."

The reporters quickly finish writing and typing in order to give Will a round of applause. Everyone loves a story of a hero's return, and this kid was serving one up on a silver platter. Will nods and smiles, accepting the sentiment. But the hope in the air fades as quickly as the sound of the applause, as Phil and Ken have to literally lift Will from his chair, and place him in a nearby wheelchair. Ted Beasley helps a very pregnant Kerry to her feet.

"Oh no. Wow," mutters Stan Greenwald as he watches Will being pushed away in his wheelchair and out of the room. "Opening Day."

He cocks his head and scribbles in his notepad.

CHAPTER 6

Will is climbing a small set of five wooden stairs that connects the floor of a local medical facility to nothing. The sweat and grimace on Will's face do not match the glacial speed at which he is ascending the stairs.

"Get up there, girl, come on now, let's go!"

Physical therapist Joseph "Joey" Gardiner, an athletic and slightly effeminate African-American man, is standing at the foot of the stairs, offering support, both physical and verbal. He shouts emphatically with a bit of a southern drawl, "Just like it's fifth down and it's the Siesta Bowl, and you are about to..."

"Wrong sport, Joe," Will interrupts, grunting with effort. "And there are only four downs in football."

"Just get your ass up the stairs!" Joey says.

Will almost smiles, and eventually makes it to the landing at the top of the small staircase.

"Great work, William! That's good," Joey says.

Will looks at the four conquered stairs below him, dejected.

"Wow. Four stairs," he says. "Someone call the Hall of Fame."

He sits down on the top stair and wipes the sweat from his brow with a towel. Joey scowls, breathes deeply, and looks Will in the eye.

"Now you listen to me, Mr. William Dobbs," he says. "You were in a coma six weeks ago. A COMA! That's like, mostly dead, do you understand? When they wheeled you in here you were like a pile of person parts, none workin'. I just watched that pathetic pile of parts walk itself up some stairs! You don't shortchange your accomplishments here, sir. That is not how we succeed. On the field, that's your house; you say whatever you want to whoever you want. But this here is my house, and you do not talk down to yourself in my house. Do I make myself CAHrystal clear?!"

"Diamond," Will says calmly.

"I said crystal, not diamond!" Joey says, confused. "Your hearing going now? What are you talkin' about?"

"Diamond. We play baseball on a diamond," says Will. "Not a field."

"Well, that seems like a tremendous waste of a precious gem," Joey answers, vexed.

Will is trying to be defiant, but can't help but smile. "When can I play?" he asks.

"Play what?" Joey asks, still miffed.

"Baseball, Joe," Will says. "Baseball."

Joey looks at Will sympathetically, and takes a seat next to him on the top stair.

"One step at a time, Mr. Dobbs," he says, "One step at a time. Keep working hard like you are, and when the time is right, hopefully you can play again."

"Hopefully?" Will says.

"Do you understand what a coma is?!" Joey yells. "Do I have to put you back in one to remind you?!"

"No. I hear you," Will says somberly. "It's just, it's not just a game to me, Joe."

"I know. It's a job. You can come work here," Joey says jokingly, trying to snap Will out of his funk. "If you trade your attitude for some gratitude."

"Thanks," Will says sadly. "No. It's not that. It's something… more."

"How did he do today?"

Will and Joey are surprised at the sudden appearance of a Kerry who has somehow waddled her sizable frame over to them, undetected.

"Hello, Mrs. Dobbs," Joey says. "And hi, Will Jr.! Your husband is doing great. Please remind him that he was recently vegetative, so, like The Police, every little thing he does is, in fact, magic." He looks at Will. "Take it slow, William. These things take time."

Will grunts, looking down at the floor.

Kerry looks at Will, proud of what he has accomplished in the short time since waking up, but concerned about how far he still has to go, and the emotional effect the ordeal is having on him. She feels lucky now, but it's also dawned on her how lucky they once were. Young and beautiful, successful, happy and healthy, with a baby on the way. That seems so long ago now.

"I don't think he can do that," she says to Joey. She looks at Will. "Can you?" she asks.

"I just want to play," Will says.

"I know. I know," she says. "Let's get you home first."

Will looks at Joey. "Should I have another go?" he asks.

"No!" says Joey. "Rest. Leave."

"OK. Bye, Joe," Will says sadly. "Thanks. See you tomorrow."

"OK," Joey says. "Behave yourself."

Will grabs two metal forearm crutches and slowly makes his way to the door. Kerry watches him go but doesn't follow him.

"Thank you," she says to Joey.

"My pleasure, Mrs. Dobbs," he says. "That's a good man you got there."

They watch Will lean his back into the door to open it, slide both crutches through and walk slowly into the parking lot.

"Will he ever play again?" she asks Joey. "Be honest."

Joey thinks for a moment. He knows the answer. He doesn't want to say it.

"I would say no," he says quietly.

Kerry is deflated.

"But," Joey continues, "if you would have asked me four weeks ago if that stubborn bastard would be walking up some stairs today, I would have said the same thing."

Kerry smiles. Joey smiles back.

"He has to," Kerry says.

"I don't think anyone can stop him," Joey says. "Even if he's running up and down the field trying to hit the ball in the basket with a big ol' crutch."

Kerry giggles and gives Joe a little hug.

"Thanks, Joe," she says. "See you tomorrow."

Joey smiles, watching her go. He picks up some towels and throws them in a bin across the room.

"Five points," he says proudly.

Will sits outside in the passenger seat of the car. He pulls out his phone and scrolls through a number of pictures until he reaches the one of him in the arms of the man in the

Yankees hat. He looks at it for a moment, then scrolls through his contacts, finds the one he is looking for, and dials.

"Hey, Al. It's Will. Yeah, hey man, everything is great… you? That's good, good. Actually, I was wondering something. You said your brother knows a bunch of NYPD detectives, right? Right. Any who specialize in missing persons?"

CHAPTER 7

The stadium is reverberating with the excitement of fifty thousand Yankee fans who have come out to see a game on a late September afternoon. Will sits watching from a glass enclosed VIP booth. Kerry and Will's parents are with him. It's the seventh inning and the Yankees are losing to the Boston Red Sox, 6-3. A ground-out by the Yankees' new third baseman ends the inning.

"All right, all right, here we go! Let's get some insurance!" says Andrew Dobbs, clapping his hands.

Will looks at him. "Who are you rooting for anyway?"

"I told you," Andrew answers. "When you are on the Yankees, I'm a Yankee fan, when you aren't, Bosox baby! Woohoo!"

Kerry and Stephanie giggle. Will sneers at Andrew.

"I'll make you a Yankee fan again soon, old man," Will says. Andrew smiles.

"Here we go, Sox!" he says, still clapping.

"Last time I get you VIP tickets," Will says with a smile. Lester Lowe's booming voice emanates from the stadium's PA system:

"Ladies and Gentlemen, your attention please. We have a very special guest in attendance tonight..."

"Ooh, here we go, Will," Kerry says, nervously licking her hand and smoothing Will's hair.

"Eew, stop it. I'm fine," he says.

"Sorry. I'm nervous." Kerry says.

"Don't be. Just wave and smile," says Will.

"When?" she asks.

"You'll know," he says.

"Yankee fans, if you would please direct your attention to the Jumbotron and give a big Yankee welcome—to Will Dobbs!"

The crowd erupts in a tumult of wild cheers and applause as they see Will and Kerry on the Jumbotron. Kerry, startled by the noise, lifts a hand and waves.

"Oh, my goodness," Kerry says, overwhelmed by the response of the crowd. She even sees fans in Red Sox gear cheering.

"It's his first time back in the stadium since that pitch put him in a coma for eight weeks," Lester says. "It is truly great to see you back. Let's hear it for Will and his wife Kerry!"

As Will and Kerry wave and take in the love from the crowd, Lester and Archie switch gears and resume their television broadcast. "He's hearing it from the crowd," says Archie. "Man, that is awesome. Let's be honest, they didn't love his bat when he was playing, but he's a good, solid kid, and everybody loves a comeback. I'm sure they would love to see him in pinstripes again. Any word on that possibility, Les?"

"We have been trying to get intel on that," Lester answers, "but it's a bit of a mystery. Dobbs himself keeps saying he'll be here next year, but Yankee brass isn't saying a thing."

"I guess we wait and see," says Archie. "Well, the Yanks aren't going anywhere near the playoffs this year, so hopefully spring training brings Dobbs, and a much-needed shot in the arm to this team."

"Amen to that," says Lester. "OK, here we go. Hanson on the mound for the Yankees…"

After the game, as the crowd is filing out and heading home after another disappointing Yankee defeat, Will is in the clubhouse getting hugs and high fives from his teammates, who are dressed in street clothes and heading home as well. He is using his forearm crutches for support. The last player gives him a hug and leaves.

"See you in Tampa," Will says.

Will is alone now, and he looks around the empty clubhouse, and slowly walks to his old locker. He tries the drawer. It opens easily.

"Got that fixed for ya," Tony says.

Will turns, sees Tony and smiles. "It only took me nearly getting killed. How are you, Tony?"

"Oh, I'm good," he says. "How you feelin'?"

"Eh, you know. Getting better every day. Not quite ready for Opening Day, I don't think. Unless they let me hit with one of these."

Will looks down at his crutches. Tony tries to change the subject.

"How's your wife?" he asks.

"She's good," Will says. "Baby boy's getting ready to meet us all."

"It's a boy?" Tony asks, smiling.

"Yep," says Will. "Baby boy."

"Well, congratulations," Tony says.

"Thanks." Will takes a moment and looks around the empty clubhouse. "I'm coming back, Tony."

"That's what I hear."

"Does anyone around here believe me?" asks Will.

Tony thinks for a moment. "No," he says.

"I have to," says Will.

"I know you think you do," says Tony.

"I don't think, I know," says Will tersely. "You don't know why. No one does."

"All right," Tony says, finding an invisible smudge to wipe off a nearby table.

"Sorry," says Will. "I just… this wasn't supposed to happen, you know? I finally got it all figured out, did everything I needed to do, and then this."

Will touches the small scar on his temple. Tony looks at him sadly.

"Will," he says, putting down his rag. "I want to tell you something, 'zat OK?"

"Sure," Will says.

"I used to play. I can't anymore. I wish I could tell you, like people do in books and movies and stuff, that I eventually learned that life is about more than baseball, but I can't. I miss playing every goddamn day. Since I been out, I watched every game on TV and read every article I could get my hands on. It's in our blood. If I could turn back time, I would. I could tell you right here, right now, that there is more to life than baseball, and that you should stop fighting to get back to playing again, and get on with your life, but I won't. Know why?"

"Why?" Will asks.

"'Cuz I want to see you play again."

Will looks at Tony and smiles. "You will, Tony. You will." He extends his hand. Tony shakes it.

"See you in the spring," Will says.

"Yes. Yes, you will," says Tony.

The men share a nod, and Will heads toward the door as Tony gets back to work.

CHAPTER 8

Will sits anxiously on a black, well-worn but expensive looking leather couch in the office of former NYPD detective Malcolm Pruitt. His crutches are leaning on the couch next to him. Pruitt sits on a chair across from Will. Tan and tall with a mop of curly blond hair and lanky build, Pruitt looks more like a surfer or struggling actor than a detective. His family moved to New York from San Luis Obispo, California when he was two, and his brothers in blue used to rib the kid from Prospect Heights for trying to hang on too desperately to his barely planted left coast roots. They even nick-named him "Bodhi." Beach bum looks aside, Pruitt had served fifteen years on the force, then ten in private business, and garnered quite the reputation as one of Gotham's best private investigators. His specialty is missing persons.

"Thanks for coming in, Will," he says.

"Of course," Will says. "What did you find out?"

"Well. I'm a straight shooter, Will, and I get the feeling you appreciate that."

"I do."

"I didn't find your father. I'm sorry. I know how much it means to you."

Will takes a deep breath. He wants to hear more, but he also wants to get out of there as soon as possible, so as not to cry in front of a tough old ex-cop.

"I understand, I knew it was a long shot," he says quickly. "I appreciate your trying. Send me any bills for whatever I owe you." Will gets up and holds out his hand to shake Pruitt's.

"Well, hold on now," the investigator says. "First off, there are no bills. Your down payment more than covered my expenses, and then some, since like I said, I sorta hit a brick wall in the search. Now, I didn't find your dad, but I do have some information you might want to know."

Will settles back into his seat again.

"What's that?" he asks.

"Well, I'll email you a full report on who he was, what he did, et cetera, a lot of which you already know from the research you've done over the years. But this was interesting," Pruitt says as he shuffles through some papers on his desk. "Everyone knows about all the data collection that's been going on lately—government, big corporations, social media, et cetera. I'm not a huge fan personally, but it does help in my line of work occasionally. International governments recently combined some of their databases. Census type data. I've got a team of geeks here and in Berlin who can access that database, crunch the digits, and find out some interesting stuff."

"Is that legal?"

"I'm not entirely sure," Pruitt says with a dismissive shrug. "I won't tell if you don't."

"OK," Will says, his interest rising. "Like, what kind of stuff?"

"Well, for one thing," Pruitt says. "Death records of basically everyone… well everyone dead anyway, for the past seventy-five years."

"Oh," Will says, dejected. "He's dead. OK."

"Well, Will, let me tell you," he says as he locates a file in a folder and scans it. "It's a pretty comprehensive data base, and I'd say with ninety-nine percent confidence, from the information you provided us, that unless your father died in Antarctica or Mozambique before 2007, he's still alive."

As these words land in Will's ears, his eyes widen.

CHAPTER 9

"Come on, sweetie! Doing great. Keep breathing!" Will says to Kerry, who is in the final stages of delivering their baby boy. The room is full of people, and it is apparent that there will be one more in it very soon. Will and a few nurses are encouraging Kerry, and the doctor is in position to "receive" at the foot of the hospital bed. Will is standing by Kerry's head, with the help of his metal crutches.

"Christ, is it a baby hippo?!!" Kerry yells. "Fuuuuuuu!!!"

"OK, doing great," the doctor says as he readies himself. "OK, time to push again. Hard. Big one, here we go…"

"UUUUNNGGHHHHNNNNGGHHH!!!!!"

Will tucks a crutch under one arm and strokes Kerry's hair. "Good! I love you. You got it. Good girl. Almost there."

"HHHRRRUNGGHHHHMMMM!!

As William Dobbs Jr. enters the room, the doctor chimes in, "OK, OK, and… good!"

He holds up the crying baby boy. He brings him to an exhausted but elated Kerry. She takes Will Jr. in her arms and gently holds him against her.

Will looks down at his son. "Oh my God," he says quietly.

Kerry's eyes are locked on baby William. "Hi baby. Hi, little Will. Hello, beautiful."

"Hello, beautiful boy," Will says. "I love you." He looks up at Kerry. "And I love you." He gives her a soft kiss on her head.

"Congratulations. You are parents," the doctor says.

"Can we hold him a minute?" Kerry asks.

"Of course. He looks perfect. We'll get him cleaned up and weighed in a minute. Take your time."

After a moment of marveling at their wiggling, crying son, Will says, "Give him to me, Kerry."

Kerry looks apprehensively at Will, who's standing while supporting much of his weight on his crutches. She's been too preoccupied to know when he last sat down. She says with an inflection of combined sadness and the protective instinct of a new mother, "Will…"

Will, with some effort, removes the crutches and leans them on the bed, and stands up straight, and steady. "I'm OK. I'm good. Just for a second. I promise."

Will holds out his arms. A nurse raises an eyebrow and surreptitiously slides a step closer behind Will, ready to catch him, or the baby, should the need arise. Kerry hesitantly and carefully hands baby William to him. Will takes him, and holds him tight, cradling him in his arms. His legs remain steady and strong.

"I gotcha. I gotcha. My boy."

Will Jr.'s cries soften as Kerry beams with joy.

CHAPTER 10

It's February in Tampa. The Yankee brass have gathered for the first day of spring training. Owner Ted Beasley and PR Chief Ken Albrecht are sitting in a front row of the stands. Normally, they wouldn't all attend, but there is someone in whose first workout they are keenly interested.

"Knock a few to third, Fletch," Manager Phil Taylor says from near home plate to an assistant coach who's hitting grounders to the infielders.

There are seven reporters sitting in the stands, about five more than usually attend the annual MLB spring kickoff, also interested in the young Yankee about to field some practice shots. Stan Greenwald is there, jotting away. All eyes are on Will Dobbs, as the ground balls head his way. They watch as Will effortlessly collects hit after hit, corralling the grounders in his glove and tossing them one by one over to first. Phil whispers to the coach at bat.

"Yank one down the line," he says.

The coach nods and proceeds to launch a wormburner right at the third base bag. Will reacts like a pinstriped panther, springing and diving headlong toward the small round projectile, his glove thwarting its singular mission with a decisive "thwap!" He scrambles to his feet and fires a laser shot across the diamond to the first baseman, sending the imaginary runner back to his imaginary place in the dugout. The team claps and offers up 'waytogoes' and 'attaboys' all around. Phil and the rest of the Yankees management give each other subtle nods and looks of approval.

"All right, let's grab some bats!" Phil bellows.

As the players leave the field to grab their bats, batting coach Al Gianfranca waddles up to Will. Al, who grew up playing stickball on the streets of the South Bronx, was a member of the Church of Baseball, attended the University of Baseball, played in the big leagues for a few years and then took up a thirty-year career as a coach. Al is old, round, Italian and grumpy. His grumpiness seems to be attributable to his existence amongst other humans, but he loves baseball, and the guys who play.

"Dobbs!" he barks at Will at the bat rack.

"Yeah, Al, what's up?"

"Now listen, Dobbs," he says. "You're gonna be back in the box soon. Just relax up there. This isn't so much a tryout as an experiment to see, you know, how your recovery is going. From your fielding, I'd say pretty friggin' good. But hitting… take your time. I'm no psychology doctor, but I imagine you got some emotional stuff still going on up there in your cranium after that crack in the melon you took. See how it feels first time back at the plate. Take it slow. It will be fine. Capisce?"

Will grabs a bat and gets a feel for it in his hands. As guileless as Al's psychoanalysis may have been, Will appreciates the effort.

"Gotcha, Al," he says.

"All right. Good."

"Hey, Al?"

"Yeah, Dobbs?"

"What was I batting back then?"

"Two eleven," says Al.

Will contemplates this for a moment, pursing his lips and nodding his head.

"Can't get much worse than that, right?"

Al's jaw drops to say something, then closes into a scowl. Will smiles at him.

Manager Phil Taylor yells across the infield, "Dobbs! OK, kid, you're up." Will heads toward home plate as Al gives him a friendly smack.

"Friggin' kids," Al mutters to himself.

Will steps up to the plate. Phil addresses the team, the coaches, the reporters, who have begun to bristle with anticipation.

"Now everyone, take this easy. Dobbs, don't try to impress us with nuclear bombs quite yet, you been through a lot to say the least, got it? Just see if you can make contact." Will nods. Phil continues, "Whatever happens, we are all glad you are here and not in a friggin' hospital, and you should be too, OK? A lot of folks watching," he continues, gesturing to the reporters, "So everybody keep cool." The players all nod. "OK, Will, let us know when you are ready," he leans forward slightly and looks Will in the eye, "Take. Your. Time."

Will nods again. "Here we go," he tells himself. He takes a moment to settle in and get comfortable. "OK, feeling good," he thinks. He looks to the pitcher. There's a quick flashback of the last pitch he faced, then the impact of the car accident. He shakes it off and takes a deep breath. Everyone is watching, all wondering, all hoping. Will indicates that he is ready with a nod to the pitcher, who winds, and delivers.

Something happens.

Will sees the entire delivery as if in slow motion; the ball that leaves the pitcher's hand is slow, large, looming. An eighty-mile-per-hour fastball reduced to a gently tossed beach ball. Will sees the rotation of the ball, the path it has taken, and will take, on its journey from the pitcher's hand to home plate. He reads the brand name and logo as clearly as if it were in his own hand. He counts the rotations of the ball, and sees the subtly changing angles of the laces as the ball turns in flight. A telling blue-ish glint flashes in Will's eye as he begins his swing. His face is a combination of excitement and focused fury. Will homes in as the ball approaches striking range. The impact is sharp. Solid. Definitive. All heads follow the soaring arc of the ball's path. The ballpark is not nearly large enough to contain the force of Will Dobbs' mighty return. The reporters are standing, too stunned to write. The team is silent as the ball settles to rest, somewhere deep in the upper deck of the Yankees' training stadium. A swell of cheers from the team slowly grows. All eyes are on Will.

Will stands in the batter's box, looking out where the ball has come to rest after its long voyage. He looks around at the cheering team mates and coaches.

"Maybe I should get beaned more often," he says.

"All right. I guess you are feeling OK," Phil says, trying to remain emotionless. "Back to work, gents." He gestures to the pitcher. "Richie, give him another."

The pitcher delivers. Another swing of Will's bat sends another ball into oblivion. The team goes crazy. Will is happy, albeit a bit shocked and confused. Something has happened to him. He feels different, better than before. He's not sure what's going on, but he likes it. The team is laughing and dancing and celebrating. The reporters start frantically writing and typing. Owner Ted Beasley addresses the onlookers from his field level seat.

"OK, all right, everyone relax," he says. "Guess they were serving Wheaties in the hospital. OK, Richie, Dobbs seems warmed up, turn it up a little."

The pitcher delivers. Once again, Will effortlessly knocks it far over the outfield wall. His teammates are laughing and hooting in amazement. Will shrugs and smiles. Phil, now with a serious look, nods to the pitcher to go again. He does, bringing the speed up to near ninety miles per hour. The ball leaves the yard again. Phil nods again. Another pitch, another homer. Will just stares in disbelief. As each moon shot is launched, the team's exhilaration turns from stunned amazement, to silent confusion. The reporters abandon their pads and laptops and pull out their phones. Will hits the next pitch out to a silent, stunned crowd.

Stan Greenwald, who has been videotaping the proceedings on his phone, breaks the silence. "What… the fu…?"

Al rushes at the reporters as fast as his squat legs will carry him. He doesn't know what is going on with Will Dobbs, but he knows that whatever it is, a bunch of nosey news jockeys weren't going to help the situation.

"All right, outta here you guys!" he shouts at the reporters. "Time to go! Out!"

"Wait, you can't—" Stan protests.

"The hell I can't," hollers Al. "I've had craps bigger than you nerds. Get out!"

Al starts grabbing the braver, or possibly slower reporters by the collars and hauling them off the field.

"Hey!" Stan shouts in protest. "You can't… have you ever heard of the Bill of Rights? Freedom of the press?! The U.S. Constitution?!"

"I don't know about no Constitution," Al answers, "but you sure as hell are going to have some constipation if I jam my foot up your ass as far as I'm about to. Get it out of here, right now!"

The reporters scurry off out of the stadium. The story isn't worth the damage that one angry Italian bull person might inflict upon them.

"We are going to find out," Stan shouts. "We will find out what's going on here!"

"Get out, you little geeks!" Al says, and waddles back to his team.

With the press gone, everyone's attention returns to Will. Ted Beasley has left his seat and joins Will at home plate.

"You OK, son?" the owner asks him with a bit of harshness and concern in his voice.

"Fine. Good," Will says. "I feel good."

Ted looks at Phil Taylor and nods toward the bull pen area. Phil understands what his boss is asking for. He whistles and waves toward the bull pen.

Yankee ace Zach Hanson, an ego as strong as his fastball, trots onto the field and takes his place on the mound. He looks hesitantly at Will.

"I don't think batting practice is in my contract, coach," he says to Phil.

"For twenty million a year you can be a team player, ya prima donna!" yells Ted. "Now pitch!"

Hanson begins to speak, then thinks better of it. He picks up a rosin bag and throws it down defiantly. An assistant coach brings a basket of fifteen balls and sets it on the mound next to Hanson. He reluctantly grabs one and sets. Will gets ready in the box, as Ted and the coaches step back to watch.

"Let's see what you got, Freakenstein," Hanson says.

Hanson sets, winds and delivers fourteen times. Fourteen balls are redirected out of the park. Hanson picks up the last one, and instead of pitching it, throws it to the ground and storms off. Will, along with the team, stand silently in disbelief.

Phil takes off his hat, rubs his head as if it would help make sense of this, and addresses the team.

"Nobody friggin' tells anyone. Got it?"

A few players nod sheepishly. Others are still frozen in mild shock. Ted Beasley walks over to Will.

"Nice hitting, kid."

"Thanks, boss," Will says meekly. "Didn't mean to freak everyone out."

"Mind telling us what the hell is going on?"

"I have no idea," Will says. "Really. I just seem to be able to hit a lot of home runs."

"I can see that," Ted says. "My office in fifteen."

"Yes, Mr. Beasley."

"And get your agent on the phone."

Will smiles warily.

"OK, guys, let's call it a day," Phil shouts. "Good work today. We're gonna get… this all… sorted out."

As Will takes the short drive from the stadium to the hotel, he's thrilled and somewhat terrified of the conversation he's about to have with his wife, who's staying there with Will Jr. this week. How exactly do you sound sane when offering up information such as, 'Hey, hon, now that I'm out of that coma, there are these superpowers we should discuss…' How does one segue into that conversation item, exactly? 'Chicken for dinner sounds great. Oh, and I can hit every pitch out of the ballpark.' Will parks his car, takes a deep breath and heads up to the room. Kerry and Will Jr. greet him at the door.

"Hey, how's my favorite guy?" he says. "And my favorite girl?"

He kisses them both.

"We are great," says Kerry. "I got your text, things went well? You feel OK?"

"I feel great," Will says. "Sorry I'm late, there was a big meeting after practice. I am so glad you are here. We need to talk."

"Everything OK?"

"Yes. Great. I think."

Kerry looks at him hesitantly. "OK," she says. "Lemme put this little man down and we can talk. Until he's hungry again anyway."

Will gives Will Jr. a kiss. Kerry goes into an adjoining room with their son in her arms. Will is nervous and excited. He doesn't know what exactly is going on in his brain and body. He likes it as much as he doesn't understand it. He sits down on the couch and clicks on the TV. The local news is on. The anchorman is reporting the top story of the evening.

"Rumors are flying out of Yankees training camp today, regarding the return of Will Dobbs, the young infielder who was hit by a pitch last season, and many thought would never play again."

"Oh boy," Will mutters.

"But not only is he out of a coma and playing here in Tampa with the Yanks, he's apparently hitting like no one can believe. Stan Greenwald from The Post is with us. Stan, tell us what you saw."

Will watches in dismay, as shaky cell phone video of him knocking balls out of the park that afternoon fills the TV screen. Stan's voice on the phone provides the play by play.

"To say that third baseman Will Dobbs is back would be the understatement of the century. This video I shot today shows him hitting six balls in a row out of the park."

On the TV screen, Al Gianfranca heads straight toward the camera, lets out a few bleeped utterances and then the video shakes violently and cuts out.

Stan continues, "As you can see, we were unceremoniously dismissed from the field just as Will was putting on a hitting display the likes of which I have never seen."

Kerry returns and stands behind Will. He's too engrossed in the newscast to notice.

"Six in a row?! You don't say, Stan. Amazing. Did you get any info on what was going on? Did you get to talk to Will?"

"No one got to talk to anyone," Stan says, "One minute we were there and the next we were kicked out. But believe you me, I will get to the bottom of this."

"What do you think is going on, Stan?" the anchor asks.

"Well, I'm as glad to see the kid return as anyone, but I almost can't believe what I saw. He was making contact like he was hitting a beach ball with a tennis racquet and launching them out of the park like it was a bazooka. I have no evidence, but I'm sure that the kid is cheating somehow."

"Are you saying he's taking some sort of performance enhancing drug?" the newscaster asks, all teeth and choreographed concern.

"Well, you know what they say," Stan says. "If it looks like a duck, quacks like a duck..."

"Will?" Kerry says.

Will, startled, turns, and clicks off the TV.

"Kerry, hey," he says as he gets to his feet and pulls a sheet of paper from his pocket and unfolds it.

"Will, what's going on?"

"I will tell you everything," he says. "The first thing you need to know is that I am officially back on the team."

Kerry does not look happy, and Will understands why. The local news was not the medium by which he envisioned the day's events reaching his wife. He suddenly found himself on the defensive, doing damage control, and he hadn't even gotten to the weird stuff yet.

"That's great, Will. But drugs? Steroids?" she says.

Will hands her the paper in his hand.

"What is this?" she asks.

"Drug test. They made me take a preliminary one on the spot after batting practice today."

Kerry grimaces and looks at Will skeptically, takes the paper from him and looks it over.

"It says negative, for everything," she says, quickly scanning to the bottom of the page. "Even alcohol."

"Ker, I wouldn't know where to get PEDs even if I wanted to take them," he says. "I'm not on anything." He takes her hands in his and looks into her eyes. "I swear."

"Well, then why would that reporter make up the story about you hitting every pitch out of the park?" she asks, still confused. "Why would he lie like that?"

"Well," Will says meekly, "he didn't, exactly."

"I heard him say you hit six home runs in a row."

"Well, yeah, that part isn't exactly true."

"I didn't think so," Kerry says, somewhat relieved. "Tell me what happened."

"Well," Will proceeds with the utmost caution, "after the reporters left, I hit a few more out."

Kerry's expression changes from confusion to concern. She drops Will's hands and sits down on a chair.

"A few?" she asks. "As in?"

"A few," says Will, his voice sounding like he is walking on a frozen lake not knowing how thick the ice or deep the water underfoot. "Like, maybe fourteen more."

Kerry's eyes widen. She's not sure how to feel, but she feels the blood rushing to her head and her ears are tingling. Something is going on with her husband that sounds more like a comic book plot than real life.

"You hit twenty home runs? Today? In a row?"

"Yes," Will says quietly.

"How did you do that, William?"

Kerry and Will stare silently at each other. Will sits down next to Kerry and takes her hand.

"Kerry, I love you. And I swear to God when I say… I don't know. I really don't. Something has happened to my brain, my eyes, my whole body. I can see the ball like it's in slow motion. It's all so clear, my eyes see it, and my brain tells my body exactly how to hit it anywhere I want to. It's like, it's like I can't not hit a home run."

"I want you to go to a doctor," Kerry says.

"The team doctors checked me out. They found nothing. I'm one hundred percent healthy."

"Come on, Will, of course they said that. There is something very strange going on and as much as I appreciate what the Yankees are doing for you, they are seeing dollar signs. I want you to go to a real doctor. Not a baseball doctor."

"I will, Kerry."

There is another long silence before Kerry continues.

"I'm scared, Will," she says. "This is weird."

Will looks at his wife. He didn't know how she would react to the incredibly strange news, but her response reminds Will why he fell in love with her, and that he will love her forever. She has one thing on her mind, above all else—his well-being. While he has been speculating about his place on the Yankees and in baseball history and the whereabouts of his birth father, Kerry is looking out for him.

"Come here," he says. He kisses her forehead. "I feel fine, Kerry. Better than ever, and I'm not saying that just because I want to play. Of course I want to play, but if there is something wrong with me, I will stop."

"Good," she says.

"But, if there isn't, I'm not going to stop playing just because I can hit every pitch out of the park."

"It's not normal, Will."

"Neither is being in a coma for eight weeks and then playing third base for a major league team a few months later.

None of this is normal. Just making the big leagues isn't exactly 'normal.' It's a one in a million chance. Maybe this is another one. Let's embrace it, Kerry. It felt so good just to make contact again Ker, I can't even explain it. Kerry, I could be the best ever. The best. Ever."

She looks him in the eyes. The joy she sees in them, doesn't bring her any comfort. "I'm just worried, Will."

"About what?"

"I don't even know. I just am."

"Don't be. This is good. It's going to all work out. This is really good."

Will pulls out another piece of paper from his pocket and hands it to Kerry. She looks at it.

"What's this?"

"My new contract. Amended. With contingencies."

"But why? You had a good contra—"

Will cuts her off by pointing to a figure at the bottom of the page. Kerry's eyes move down and when they land on the number, widen more than when she heard about the twenty home runs. She looks up at Will, shocked. He shrugs.

CHAPTER 11

The next day, there is a noticeably larger cadre of reporters in the press section of the Tampa stadium. Workouts are going on normally, the Yankees taking their rounds of batting practice. The reporters are all poised, all waiting for the same thing—laptops open and ready, Stan Greenwald's pen firmly in his grasp. Will is doing some stretches near the dugout. The player at bat flies one out to left field, where it is caught by a coach and tossed back in. Al Gianfranca addresses the team.

"OK, guys, let's bring it in. Some sprints and then call it a day."

The reporters all rise from their seats and begin shouting at Al.

"What the hell, Al?" yells Stan. "When's Dobbs batting?"

"He's not today," Al says gruffly. "Don't you worry about it."

Stan harrumphs in disgust. "So, I'll just write, Will Dobbs returns to Yankee lineup but doesn't need batting practice anymore."

"I didn't say that," snarls Al. "He's just not feeling up to it."

Stan holds up his pen and pad and feigns writing in it. "Will Dobbs has mystery injury that allows him to field, but not hit," he says.

Al is getting increasingly frustrated with Stan and the other grumbling reporters.

"I didn't say that either you—"

"Al," Yankee PR chief Ken Albrecht interrupts from behind his iPad. He touches his breast pocket. Al, his face showing signs of frustrated compliance, pulls out a crumpled piece of paper from his breast pocket and reads, "Will Dobbs has made a full recovery from the injury sustained last season. We are very pleased to have him on the team once again. We look forward to this season. Please join us Opening Day to see Will's return to the game." He shoves the paper back in his shirt pocket.

"Ahh, that's corporate bull and you know it, Al," Stan says. "What the hell is going on?!"

"That's all I got guys," says Al. "See you tomorrow."

"Will we see Dobbs bat?" Stan asks.

Al looks at him, then at Ken Albrecht. Al opens his mouth to say something, thinks better of it, waves his hands in a dramatic Italian flourish indicating his displeasure with the entire situation, and turns and walks away. Ken Albrecht's eyes go back to his iPad.

"We're gonna find out, Al," Stan says. "We are. Or at least, I am."

CHAPTER 12

Mid-morning thunderstorms have cleared over the Bronx, and Opening Day at Yankee Stadium is about to get underway. The always electric first-game crowd is noticeably more so this year. There are an inordinate number of "Dobbs" jerseys on the backs of the faithful. Rumors about the young infielder back from a coma have been flying for months, and now everyone is here to see what all the buzz is about.

Kerry is in the crowd, sitting in a VIP area with Will's parents. Little Will is home with a sitter. Kerry is worried and excited. Even though she is pretty sure she knows what she is about to see, she is still pensive, and more subdued than a wife about to see her husband's heroic return to baseball should be. Despite the clouds overhead dispersing, it feels dark. Dark and strange.

Stan Greenwald is at his designated post in the press area. He's become a bit of a reluctant internet sensation, with the video he shot of Will Dobbs getting nearly a billion hits on YouTube. Despite the public's thirst for information, Stan has been battling Yankee gatekeepers since that day in Tampa, trying to get info on Will, and receiving none. Will never took batting practice after that first day, not in public anyway, and he didn't play in any pre-season games. The only pertinent information the Yankees released to the press on the matter were the results of five independent drug testing labs, all coming to the same unanimous conclusion—Will Dobbs was using no performance enhancing drugs whatsoever. Stan has seen a lot in his thirty years reporting, and he's never seen anything like this. But it has a smell he's keenly familiar with—fishy.

Tony watches the proceedings on a monitor in the clubhouse. He's heard the rumors of Will's mysterious home run hitting powers. He wants his return to be a triumphant one; but if these rumors are true, it's going to be a lot more than that.

"Well, folks, here we go," announcer Lester Lowe says to what is undoubtedly one of the largest audiences in the history of televised sport, "It's Opening Day here in Yankee stadium, but the story today isn't about the Yankees, or the Blue Jays for that matter. It's about one man—the young third baseman from Beantown, Will Dobbs."

"Too true, Les, too true," color commentator Archie Talbot says. "He got hit by a pitch that nearly killed him early last season, and now he's back. But this isn't just a return to glory story. It's a bit more than that, isn't it, Les?"

"Absolutely. There have been some really bizarre rumors about Dobbs' newfound hitting abilities coming out of Tampa this spring. The Yanks have been tight-lipped and there was basically a press lock-out down there. So, no one really knows what's going on, but everyone sure as shootin' wants see for themselves! And that's going to happen, Arch, right here, right now."

"It's been a strange spring for sure, Les, and all I can say is I am looking forward to this game! They have Dobbs batting first, which is unexpected, so we will find out soon enough. Here we go, first pitch coming up!"

The Blue Jays bat, but it almost feels like a formality. After a lead-off single, the next three batters go down quickly.

"OK, Will Dobbs up for the Yanks," Les announces over the deafening roar of the crowd. "I guess all that's left to do is watch."

Will steps up to the plate. He tips his cap to a crowd sizzling with excitement. Even the opposing Blue Jays give a quick round of applause in honor of his return.

Will feels honored and happy. He's back. Where he's supposed to be. Playing the game he loves, and doing what he is meant to do. He's got a second chance and making all of his dreams come true. As he steps into the box, he looks around at the thousands of faces in the crowd.

"Let's play ball!" The umpire shouts. Will continues to scan the crowd, thinking.

Where are you… where are you…

"StrIIIIIIIIIKE!!!!!" the umpire calls as the ball sails directly through the center of the strike zone and thumps the leather of the catcher's glove.

The crowd goes… the crowd doesn't know what to do. Or think. Kerry and Will's parents are similarly confounded. Will looks a bit confused himself. Or nervous. He hasn't been in front of a crowd this size since the coma. He kicks some dirt and settles in. Al Gianfranca looks at Coach Taylor.

"Well that was… a strike," he says. "Definitely in there." He looks at Will who seems stiff and uncomfortable. "What in the…"

So many people… so many fathers.

"StEEEEEErike two!!!"

Al and Phil Taylor exchange looks, and Phil gestures to an assistant to start looking at the active roster on the wall. From the press booth, Stan starts furiously writing in his notepad. A strange rumble begins to roil in the crowd. The pitcher smiles triumphantly. Will shakes his head, calls for time, and tries to focus and settle into his stance.

"You OK, Dobbs?" the umpire asks.

After a moment, Will takes a deep breath and says, "Yes. Fine. All good. Ready."

The pitcher sets again, and delivers.

Will's eyes twinkle. He sees the ball leaving the pitcher's hand… floating helplessly toward him, as elusive as a lumbering elephant. His mouth curls into a slight smile as he swings. The crack is sharp, and loud. The pitcher is no longer smiling. The ball is traveling skyward toward the stands beyond the center field wall in a tremendous hurry. The crowd is going insane, finally witness to the mysterious athletic abilities of young William Dobbs. The ball lands in the middle deck of seats amongst a frenzy of fans, all trying to get their hands on what just became one of the world's most valuable baseballs.

"Well, that just happened," says Lester Lowe.

Al and Phil breathe a sigh of relief, and smile broadly as the entire Yankee team jumps to its feet to cheer. Tony looks on proudly from the clubhouse, as Will takes off toward first. Stan shakes his head as he writes.

Will rounds the bases, trying to act normal though his heart is racing. He crosses home and arrives at the dugout, where the team is there to greet him. He accepts their hugs and high-fives and attempts to descend into the dugout, but the crowd won't have it. They continue cheering until he comes out and tips his cap. He finds Kerry and blows her a kiss.

Will looks around the crowd.

Where are you…

CHAPTER 13

The next day's edition of the New York Post lands on editor Leo Folcher's desk with a smack. He looks up at a scowling Stan Greenwald and shrugs. Besides a relatively neat desk, the editor's office doesn't look like it's been redecorated, or cleaned, since around 1980. Will Dobbs' picture is on the front cover of the paper, along with the headline "WELCOME BACK BOMBER." The story is on the back cover as well. The Yankees won the season opener 10-3. Stan is shouting emphatically at Leo.

"Four at-bats, four home runs, Leo," he says. "Four!"

"I know. I know," says Leo. "Everyone knows."

"Something is going on here, Leo. Something's not right."

Leo leans back in his big leather desk chair, notices something that could be edible on a shelf behind him. Without getting up, he grabs it, sniffs it, and puts it in his mouth. Stan frowns.

"Stan, he got drug tests done by the five most renowned facilities in the United States and Canada," Leo says, "And that lab in England that figured out that the Croatian Olympic women's curler actually belonged on the men's team. Dobbs is clean. They tested him for friggin' gorilla hormones, Stan. The Yanks knew there would be questions, so they were ready with the answers. He's clean."

"Four home runs. After those first two strikes, he didn't even take another pitch. Six pitches, four home runs Leo. Four! He was in a coma less than a year ago. He didn't play any pre-season games!"

"What do you want me to say, Stan?"

"You don't think this is a story?"

"Well, yeah, it is. He's a hero."

"Hero schmeero," Stan says with disgusted resolve. "He's cheating. It's just a matter of time before he's caught. Let me write something about him cheating for tomorrow's edition. So we can say we were on it first."

"Not yet," says Leo. "It's not the story."

"You are wrong."

"Nothing would make me happier than for you to prove that. Go find the story."

"I will. Oh, I will."

CHAPTER 14

Over the next three months, Will Dobbs is everywhere. People around the world know the story of the kid who came out of a coma who can now hit every pitch out of the park. By May, he'd hit 74 homers, shattering Barry Bonds' record. By the All-Star Break he'd hit 321, breaking every home run related record there was. There is a constant murmuring amongst historian types to put an asterisk next to Will Dobbs' records, but no one can agree on what the corresponding footnote would be. Stadiums are filled to capacity everywhere Will and the Yankees play. TV ratings are higher than ever, and the manufacturers can't churn out "Dobbs" jerseys quickly enough to keep up with the demand of fans. Will's face is on the cover of every magazine, from Sports Illustrated, to Time, to Scientific American and even medical journals. The headlines read "Greatest Slugger Ever," "Can Anyone Stop Will Dobbs?" and "1000.00" His performance is baffling, mesmerizing and inspiring.

As a once proud nation struggles with her identity and values, its humanity clouded by Snapchat celebrities, sex scandals, and politics as a reality show, Will Dobbs has brought an old-fashioned human element to American pride. A superhuman element. And a wholesome one. While modern fame often seemed a temporary glow before the inevitable crash and burn, there was no jealousy in watching Will's talent, only joy. For many, it's exactly what their psyches needed to get them out of the rut of their increasingly unfulfilling existences.

When phones get smarter as people get dumber, no one argues or disagrees about history or sports statistics anymore, because all answers are literally in the palms of their hands. People had stopped talking about sports trivia and telling stories about the game. They simply Googled it. But Will changed that. You couldn't get the answer to the mystery of Will Dobbs from a website. People wanted to see him play, together, live. They discussed, argued, and speculated as to what exactly was happening. They watched the magical story of Will Dobbs, baseball, and an American hero unfold in front of their eyes. They talked, bonded, loved and wondered, just like they used to.

In a strange way, Will's fame, with its indefinable origins was more real than the false idols dominating modern American media, where it seems more people become famous for being famous than actually achieving anything worthy of fame. That wasn't the case with Will Dobbs. Even though no one was sure how he was doing it, those balls were not leaving the nation's baseball cathedrals each night due to spin doctors, PR hacks, agents, nepotism, cronyism, politics, viral videos, or slick editing. They were because of one man's ultra-human ability to hit a baseball with a bat better than any man had ever done before. Whatever was going on with this young Yankee, America, and the entire world, loved it.

Stan Greenwald, however, isn't having it. He cannot get past the one thing gnawing at his mind. This was wrong. Something was not right here. Magic is not real. No man can do what Will Dobbs is doing. People today were so used to special effects in movies, and newscasters and politicians lying to them about everything, they didn't know the difference between reality and BS anymore. They see "magic" in front of their eyes and they don't question it, they regard it as cool as the hottest trending YouTube video. Let those who need God or magic to get through the day believe in their almighty Will Dobbs, not me, Stan thought. He doesn't know how Dobbs is cheating, and he doesn't care why. He didn't even have anything against him per se, but he is not going to let there be a false God on earth in his lifetime if he could help it. Let the mindless lemmings find another God. Not a baseball player. Not in this city. Not in this stadium, where he watched Mantle, Mattingly and Jackson hit home runs. He was going to figure out what was really going on with this kid. This was cheating, pure and simple, and Stan hated cheaters. The steroid scandal rocked baseball to its core, and Stan's outlook and love of the game would never be the same again. Now that the rampant usage seemed to be under control, he wasn't going to let some kid come in and ruin it all over again. Not on his watch. He picks up his desk phone and dials.

"Hello. Is this Mrs. Dobbs? Stephanie Dobbs? It's Stan Greenwald from The Post. I know, I know, I'm sorry, I'm sure you are getting a ton of calls. I just wanted to ask a quick question. Not many people know that Will's adopted, do you know anything about his biological parents…?"

Dr. Oz is sitting in his standard place, in the modern styled white armchair on the set of his talk show. Will Dobbs is in the guest chair, taping an episode which will air later that day. He's comfortable, at this point, having done dozens of these types of interviews, between games, throughout the season. The Yankees had to hire a special media coordinator to navigate and manage Will's never-ending appearances around the games and travel.

"So, William, when you first woke up from the coma, did you feel different?" asks Dr. Oz.

"Not really. I mean I felt like sh… poop, you know."

The audience of Midwestern minivan moms laughs.

"Sorry everyone, he's had a traumatic head injury!" bellows Dr. Oz, all teeth and tan. "Head trauma can make you feel downright awful. Sure. When did you start feeling like yourself again?"

"At first, I was a mess, didn't know who I was or where I was. I didn't even recognize my wife."

The crowd lets out a collective sigh.

"I remembered her and everything pretty soon though. Then, as I started recovering, I started feeling great," Will says. "Big thanks to Dr. Emerson and his whole team, they were amazing. And Joey, my physical therapist. I mean, I had a lot to feel good about too, my wife, my new baby boy, I'm a New York Yankee. So, I just thought, wow this coming out of a coma thing feels pretty good."

"The doctors didn't think you would be in any shape to attend spring training, but you did," says Dr. Oz. "Tell us about that."

"It was weird, ya know," Will says. "Like, that first time I got up to bat, it was different. I felt like I knew I was going to hit a home run. Even before the pitcher wound up. I can't really explain it. I had a quick memory of the pitch that hit me and then something clicked. Everything, my brain, my body, everything was just totally focused. I never felt anything like that before."

Dr. Oz touches his chin and looks at Will in his most inquisitive and fascinated TV-doctorly manner. "Amazing. Remarkable," he says. "And it's the same, even now, every time you step up to bat?"

"Same thing every time," Will says. "I just know I'm gonna hit it out. I haven't been wrong yet. I can't not hit a home run. I know this will piss people off, but for me, it's easy. I don't know what exactly happened, or why it happened, but I'm gonna hit a home run every time I'm up, no matter what. It just is what it is."

"And I know you have been asked this a million times, but once more, for the record, for the entire Dr. Oz audience, no drugs?"

"Dr. Oz, before I got the fame and the fortune—"

"The seven-hundred-fifty-million-dollar, seven-year contract," Dr. Oz interrupts, as the audience lets out a subdued gasp. Will is slightly annoyed at the TV doctor's shockboating.

"Yes. Before the contract. Back then, I wasn't being invited to appear on talk shows, I was a struggling rookie from Marshfield, Massachusetts. Then I woke up from a coma and didn't know if I would walk again. I worked my butt off to be able to carry my baby boy to his crib, and hopefully play ball again someday. I only took what the doctors prescribed me. No performance enhancing drugs. None. Never have, never will. I'll take any test anyone wants to give me. Anytime."

"Got it. OK. Last question. Any progress on finding your Dad?"

Will is a bit taken aback by the question, but he answers as if he thought it might come eventually.

"Someone's done his homework," Will says.

"Stan Greenwald from the New York Post heard you were going to be on the Dr. Oz show and gave me a call," Dr. Oz says.

"Ah yes, Stan. He seems to be not enjoying my success as much as a lot of people."

The crowd chuckles and a few boos are tossed out for Stan's benefit.

"No, no," Will tells them, "He's just doing his job. Investigating, trying get to the bottom of the story. He didn't find any drugs, because there aren't any, so now he's digging for another story. Well, here it is. Sorry Stan, you're about to get scooped."

The audience is rapt. Dr. Oz is almost salivating at this career boosting moment. He's mentally tallying up potential hits on his YouTube channel. He gives his Executive Producer standing off stage one of those "Here we go!" nods.

"When I was one, I lost my parents in a car accident. I have known that I was adopted for as long as I can remember. When I was nine, I learned that my dad had actually survived the crash, and chose to give me up for adoption."

The audience gasps, and Dr. Oz's eyes widen. "Really?" he says, with possibly genuine fascination.

"Yes," Will answers. "I don't know much about my dad, but I know he was a Yankee fan. So I dreamed of making the Yankees as a way for my dad to find me. It was the only way I could think of to make contact."

"And you did it. You made the Yankees."

"Yep. I did."

The audience applauds.

"Amazing," says Dr. Oz earnestly. "But no luck with your dad yet?"

"No," Will says quietly. "And at this point, if he hasn't found me, I'm thinking he really doesn't want to. Or he can't."

Will has been living with this for years, but he never told anyone except his wife and PI Malcolm Pruitt before today. Now the Dr. Oz audience, and soon Stan Greenwald and the world would know how the superhuman saga of the Bomber from Beantown began. Sadness and relief wash over Will, as he wipes a tear from his eye. The audience sighs and lets out a collective "Awww."

"Will Dobbs!" Dr. Oz says at a volume that startles Will, the TV doctor's excitement bubbling over despite his futile attempts at suppression and compassion. "Thank you for being on the Dr. Oz Show today. We wish you all the best. Congratulations on your success, best of luck, and stay healthy. And I hope someday, even though it's a very long shot, I hope you find your dad."

"Thanks, Doc," says Will.

"William Dobbs, everyone! On tomorrow's show, Is Your Baby Psychic? See you then!"

Will waves to the cheering studio audience. He thinks to himself that even though things didn't turn out exactly how he wanted or planned, things have turned out pretty well. He's the best baseball player who ever lived. He smiles.

CHAPTER 15

Will, Kerry and Will Jr. are visiting Will's parents while the Yankees are on a road trip in Boston. Kerry and Stephanie are trying various outfits on a reluctant Will Jr. while Will and Andrew are having a drink on the deck, enjoying a cool New England summer evening.

"Stan called here again? Oh jeez," Will says. "I'm sorry."

"It's OK."

"I will make sure it doesn't happen again," Will says. "What did he want?"

"He wanted to ask about your Dr. Oz appearance. To know about your real father," Andrew says. He doesn't try very hard to hide the animosity in his voice. Andrew's bitterness toward the whole situation had been simmering really since the day he and Stephanie told Will that his dad hadn't died in the car accident. There have been times since then when Andrew wished they hadn't. He wasn't sure how his son would react at the time, and he certainly never thought it would lead to superhuman powers and a quest to find a man that he could never be, while the world watched. A man who, Andrew would never say this to Will, but as far as he was concerned, a man who did the wrong thing. He abandoned his child. He and Stephanie did the right thing, by telling Will, just as they did by adopting him and raising him to be the happy, healthy, smart man he'd become. When Carlton Rossi almost lost Will in a car accident, he abandoned him. When Andrew watched Will almost get killed playing a game, he waited day after day for the call saying if his son was awake or dead. Andrew Dobbs was a more than a little tired of Carlton Rossi getting the world's attention and sympathy.

"Dad," Will says. "You want to talk about it?"

"Not really. I just, it's just… I raised you. You were a good kid and now you're a good husband and father, and a great ball player. I bought you your first glove, I took you to all those Little League games, I watched your high school and college games, and all anyone wants to talk about is… him. No one knows who Andrew Dobbs even is. And this obsession of yours with finding him, I don't think it's healthy. What's the point? I'm proud of you and the man you've become, and Carlton Rossi had absolutely nothing to do with it. And yes, damn it, I'd like to get some credit for it. Not a ghost." Andrew finishes his beer and gets up to get another.

Will and his father had come close to having this conversation many times, but this was the first time it had all been laid out there. Will had felt a vague sort of anger toward his father regarding it. Who was he to judge Will's desire to find his real father? But now, looking at Andrew, he sees how much this desire has hurt him, the man who raised him, the man he actually loves—not Carlton Rossi, the man who he just loves the idea of finding one day.

"Dad."

"Yes, Will?"

"I love you."

"I love you, too. Sorry I'm behaving like a jealous girlfriend."

"You aren't. I get it. You are a big part of my success and it's my fault that everyone is looking at someone else as the reason for it. I'm sorry."

"It's OK, son."

"Hey Dad?"

"Yeah?"

"You're coming to the game tomorrow, right?"

"Of course."

"Still in Section 40?"

"Bleacher Creature for life."

Will smiles at his father's childlike enthusiasm for the game. He's offered VIP seats in Fenway numerous times, but Andrew always prefers to sit with "his people."

"You still have your glove?" Will asks.

"Of course."

"Bring it."

"Why?"

"Just bring it, OK."

"This is Will Dobbs' hometown, Arch," Lester Lowe says into the microphone. "But you wouldn't know it by the reaction from this crowd." Will Dobbs steps up the plate to lead off for the Yankees in this first game of the Boston road trip. The crowd is booing relentlessly. Will loves it. This is part of what being a Yankee is all about. You could gauge the quality of the season you were having by the volume of the Red Sox fans' boos directed at you. He scans the hostile crowd and tries to stifle a smile. He reveled in the jeers, but he certainly didn't want to get beaned again by a scorned pitcher. He settles into his stance and takes one more glance over the right field wall into Section 40. The pitcher winds, and delivers.

The distinctive crack of the bat signals the feverish crowd that the all too familiar result of one of Will Dobbs mighty swings is underway. The ball sails high and far toward the opposite field wall in deep right. It lands far on the other side of it—into the outstretched glove of Andrew Dobbs.

As the Jumbotron reveals the equally thrilled and stunned recipient of the titanic shot, a collective amazement stirs the crowd, shifting its anger to a strange combination of wonder and confusion.

"Isn't that…?" Archie Talbot asks.

"Yes, it is. Well, I'll be darned," Lester Lowe answers. "In an amazing… coincidence, Will Dobbs' father, who lives here in Boston, just caught that home run ball."

Will smiles broadly as he tips his cap in the direction of his dad and trots off to first base.

"Wait. Was that a coincidence?" Archie asks, as they watch Andrew high-fiving fans all around.

"I… I think so. Or, who knows? Wow. We'll be back right after this."

CHAPTER 16

Will sits at a table for two in a four-star restaurant in Manhattan. He takes a sip from his wine glass, then looks at its contents, astonished by its taste. He shrugs and smiles. Kerry returns to the table, wearing a form fitting fuchsia dress that she doesn't think fits her anymore after having Will Jr., but it does. A waiter, or napkin ninja, appears from nowhere to pull out her chair and replace the cloth napkin in her lap, in a seamlessly choreographed stealth maneuver.

"Oh," Kerry says with surprised delight. "Thank you."

The ninja responds in an accent as thick and creamy as a slice of brie, "It eez my plezzure." He then moves on to coordinate his next sneak attack on displaced linen.

"William!" Kerry says in an excited whisper. "This place is insane! There is a fish tank in the bathroom!"

"I know, right? Happy anniversary. Sorry it had to wait till the All-Star break. How's the big guy?"

"Good. The sitter just texted that he's happily asleep."

"How did people raise children before cell phones?"

"No idea. I guess you just left them wherever you needed to, and hoped they were still there when you returned."

Will smiles. It's been quite a year. Kerry had her doubts when Will's unique abilities came to light, but she seems to be settling into this new weird world of fame, fortune and superhuman home runs.

"I love you," Will says.

"I love you, too."

Just then, a couple appear at Will and Kerry's table. The husband is wearing pleated khakis, a blue blazer, and a fanny pack. The woman is real estate agent chic: too blonde, too tan, too much make-up, too much jewelry. She was pretty at one time, but not at this time. They've clearly enjoyed a good bit of New York City's finest wine.

"Mr. Dobbs. Mrs. Dobbs. We are so sorry to bother you," the wife says.

Will and Kerry exchange a look and breathe deeply in order to stay cordial.

"Sorry, yeah, we saw you from our table. It's just that our son, Jacob," the husband says, "he's, I mean you, he's your biggest fan. We're from Cincinnati, but he's a Yankee fan now."

"He just loves you," the wife says. "He never misses a game."

"Well, thanks," Will says politely. "Nice to meet you both."

"You too!" the wife says. "Oh my, I can't believe it's you!"

The ninja waiter materializes again, having caught sight of the social transgression taking place in his arena. Horrified at the tourists' behavior, he apologizes to Will with his eyes and quickly scurries over.

"Pleez madame, monsieur," he says to the tourists, his hand gently guiding the husband toward the exit, "I am glad you have eenjoyed your deener. Pleez, have a good evening."

"We will," the husband says, his Bordeaux courage kicking in. "It's just, I know you aren't supposed to, but if you could just sign something for Jake..."

"Monsieur!" pleads the waiter. "Madame, pleez!"

"It's all right," says Will, not wanting the tipsy tourist versus French firebrand situation to unduly escalate. The waiter apologizes again with his eyes.

The woman raps her husband on the arm. "Frank!"

Frank is startled into action. He fumbles in his mannypack, pulls out a "Phantom of the Opera" playbill, and a pen, and hands it to Will, who scribbles on the playbill and hands it back.

"Oh wow," says Frank, in awe. "Oh wow. Thank you so much."

"OK," says the waiter sternly. "That eez all. Have a good night."

"If we could just get a quick..." Frank says as he fumbles for a camera.

"Monsieur! I must inseest!"

"Yeah," Will says. "I'm just trying to have dinner. Really. Good night."

The wife is slightly perturbed, but says, "OK. Fine. We understand."

"Right. OK. Sorry," says the husband. "Thank you, Mr. Dobbs. Mrs. Dobbs."

"Yes. OK," says Kerry. "Have a good night."

The couple awkwardly stumbles toward the front door, half elated, half drunk, half yelling under their breath at each other about something to do with Facebook. The waiter notices a man at a neighboring table furtively recording the happenings at the Dobbs' table with a camera phone.

"REALLY?! Monsieur!" he says.

"Sorry… sorry," the man apologizes meekly as he puts the phone down.

The ninja waiter is seething. Will and Kerry are staying calm, but the entire situation is beginning to wear on them.

"I am so sorry, Madame and Monsieur. I weesh we had a more private table. The Executive Chef eez a communist. Nuhzeeng eez private!" Will and Kerry can't help but smile at the poor waiter's passionate disgust.

"It's OK," Will says. "Your restaurant is lovely."

"I shall remain witheen strikeeng deestance should anuzair plague-reeden scoundrel deeside to deesrupt your deener. Good eevening."

He bows, turns, and leaves.

"He's hardcore," Will says.

"I didn't know the French could hardcore like that," Kerry says. "I like him. Can we have one?"

"Maybe if we make it to the World Series."

Kerry smiles as she takes a sip of wine. "My God," she says.

"Good?" Will asks.

"I want to shower in this."

"It's the most expensive bottle they have. I don't know anything about wine, so that's the only way I'd know that I picked a good one."

"Will!" she laughs and playfully smacks his hand across the table. "I don't think I'll ever get used to this."

"Me neither," Will says. "Sorry about the fans. I thought we could just go out to dinner. Guess not."

"It's all right. People get excited. It's just a little… weird."

Will looks around. He notices the guy's phone is still sitting on the table.

"Hey," he says to Kerry. "Come with me."

"Where?"

"Not sure," he whispers. "Just… come on."

He takes her by the hand and guides her toward the back of the restaurant. They pass the waiter on the way.

"We'll be right back," Will says.

"Of course, Monsieur," he says.

Will sees a staircase, heading down. He leads Kerry down to the lower level of the restaurant.

"Where are we going?" Kerry asks. "The bathroom?!"

"Yes," says Will. Kerry raises an eyebrow. "No!" he says. "Here!"

They duck into a dark hallway that seems to lead to a closet or storage room. There is a door with an "Employees Only" sign on it. Will stops Kerry and gently places her back against the door. He begins to kiss her.

"I love you," he says.

"I love you, too," Kerry says, "But I'm not having sex with you in a storage closet."

Will smiles. He takes his hands from around Kerry and hold hers in his.

"That isn't why I brought you here. I just wanted to give you something and I didn't want the tourist twins or Mr. YouTube to see."

Will reaches into his pocket and pulls out a ring box.

"Will!" Kerry says.

"Happy anniversary," Will says.

He opens the box. Ten carats of canary yellow diamond are inside. Kerry gasps.

"Will!" she says. "No."

"Yes. We've been through this already. Put it on."

"No, Will. It's too much. This is too much."

Will takes the ring out and puts the box back in his pocket.

"Kerry, I love you. I want you to have it. I brought you on this crazy ride you never really asked to be on, you should at least get some great stuff along the way. Don't worry, I'm not buying yachts and helicopters or islands. Just something special for you. Again, what else am I going to spend a billion dollars on?"

"It's not a billion dollars," Kerry says.

"Three quarters," Will says. Kerry gives him a sideways look. "Kerry, we turned down a Doritos deal this morning that would have paid for twenty of these." He slides the ring onto her right ring finger. "Do you like it?"

Kerry looks at the ring and turns her hand as the giant stone catches an overhead light and glimmers like a fallen star. "Yes, Will. I mean of course. It's just… I don't need—"

"No one needs one of those, Kerry. But some people deserve one."

He kisses her on the lips.

"I love you," he says. "I'm going to take care of you and little Will forever. You have nothing to worry about."

"OK," she says.

She hugs Will tightly. She looks at the ring over Will's shoulder. She's smiling, but concern simmers deep behind her eyes.

CHAPTER 17

The All-Star game is in Washington, D.C. Will is batting lead-off for the American League. He walks toward home plate to the familiar chorus of cheers. He tips his hat to the crowd, which responds wildly. As he steps into the batter's box, the noise dies down. Will hears something he's heard many times at away games, but didn't expect at the All-Star game. Someone behind the home plate fence is booing. Loudly. Will is a little surprised and holds up a hand to take a time out and step out of the box. He glances at the 'fan,' beer and opinions flowing.

"BOOOO!! BOOO! You suck, Dobbs! You are a cheater! And a bore!! Wow, gee I wonder what's gonna happen?? Ooooohh, another boring home run. You suck!!"

"Dobbs!" barks the umpire. Will looks at him, slightly startled. "You're up, kid. Ignore that moron."

Will smiles, shrugs the guy off and steps into the box.

"Play ball!" the umpire bellows.

The pitcher delivers. Will's eye glints a little extra brightly as he grits his teeth and swings with a low grunt. The ball sails high and far over the left field wall, ending its flight at the very top of the upper deck, settling into a structural area where there aren't any seats or fans. The ball gets swallowed into the outer limits of the building. The crowd goes wild.

Stan Greenwald is in the press box chatting with another reporter.

"Jesus H, did you see that?" he says.

"I've never… that was, I've never seen a ball hit that far," the reporter answers.

"That could have been seven hundred feet," says Stan.

"Or more," the reporter says.

"What is going on with this kid?"

The crowd, sounding like maniacal thunder, watches as the ball disappears from sight. Everyone is up on their feet. Everyone, that is, except the one fan behind the home plate fence. Will looks in his direction. He's sitting, putting his hand to his mouth feigning a huge yawn. Will smirks at him, tosses his bat and heads down the line toward first. That booing fan, and the monstrous shot he hit in response, just brought out something in Will that he hasn't felt since he emerged from the coma—anger. Stan Greenwald notices a change in Will's demeanor and scribbles in his notepad.

Will enters his house after a late-night flight. Kerry is there in her pajamas to greet him.

"Hi, baby." She gives him a hug.

"Oh, you shouldn't have waited up. How's the big guy?"

"He's good, a little cranky. I just fed him. Sleeping again. I watched the game. You were great."

"Yeah," he says. Kerry immediately notices his somber mood.

"What's wrong, Will?"

"I hit four home runs. I always hit four home runs. Unless I hit five."

Kerry hasn't seen her husband sad in quite a while. She rubs his shoulder.

"Hey," she says. "I love you. The fans love you."

"One didn't, Ker. He was booing. Said I was a cheat."

"Everyone thought that at first, Will. But you're not. You know that. If that jerk still thinks you are, well he's just dumb. He's wrong. Who cares?"

"He said I was boring, Ker."

"What?" she asks, confused.

"Yeah. Boring."

"That's ridiculous. You have fans all over the world. You are an exciting player. You are an inspiration to a lot of people, especially that little munchkin upstairs. Don't let one loser get you down."

"Oh yeah, an inspiration," Will says. "They can all aspire to get a life-threatening injury that leads to them acquiring freakish powers." Kerry is taken aback by Will's sudden change in attitude. Before she can continue the conversation, Will ends it. "I'm beat," he says. "I'm gonna head to bed."

"OK," says Kerry, as she watches him go.

CHAPTER 18

"You know, when you make half million dollars a day, they have people who will do that for you."

Will turns from his locker drawer. He sees Tony and smiles.

"Hey, Tony, how ya doing? Get a couple days off?"

"Yeah. Well, one. I like to work. Great All-Star Game. You have fun?"

"Yeah, ya know."

"You played some damn good ball. Saw you turn that double play on the Benitez grounder. He's fast."

"That was cool. It's everything else I'm not sure I'm very good at."

"Hitting?" Tony says, surprised. "Yeah, you really gotta start getting it together at the plate."

"Ha," Will says.

Manager Phil Taylor pokes his head into the clubhouse. "Oh, you are here," he says to Will. "Welcome back."

"Hey, Coach," Will says. "Thanks."

"Hey, Tony," Phil says.

"Coach," he says, with a nod.

"Will," Phil says, "There's someone here to see you."

"Who is it?" Will asks.

"I uhhh… I think you should just come up to my office."

Will lights up. He leaves his stuff where it lies, jumps up and bolts out the door, practically knocking Phil over.

"Dobbs?! What the..?" Phil says.

He looks at Tony, who shrugs. Phil shakes his head and bounds after his superstar slugger.

Will reaches the office before Phil. He barges through the door, almost wild-eyed with anticipation. His excited demeanor changes when he recognizes his visitor. The others in the room have all sort of frozen, and are staring oddly at Will.

"Mr. Dobbs," Vice President Peter Mahoney says in a southern drawl, rising warily from a chair and extending his hand. "Pleasure to meet you."

Will looks around and sees Yankee owner Ted Beasley sitting in a large leather chair, aborting an attempt to light a cigar and looking up at him through a scowl, another man in a suit and glasses holding a tablet computer, and a Secret Service officer with his hand under his jacket, having become suddenly alert due to Will's somewhat bizarre and spirited entrance.

"Everything OK?" asks Vice President Mahoney.

"Oh. Yes. Sorry. Fine." says Will, surprised, disappointed and embarrassed. "Nice to meet you, Mr. Vice

President." The secret service agent calmly assumes "at ease" attitude. Will shakes the Vice President's hand.

"Jeez, Will, big fan?" says Ted Beasley with a good natured snide smile as he lights his cigar. "I wouldn't have picked you for a Democrat!" He winks at the Vice President.

"No. I mean, yes." says Will. "I just thought you were… no… It's really nice to meet you. Are you staying for the game?"

"Yanks-Sox? Sure as hell am! Lotsa bigwigs in town after the break. Celebs, fat cats, hot shots and politicos like me are coming in. Coming to see you, I imagine."

"Ahh," scoffs Will. "Not much to see."

"The Bombastic Bomber from Beantown?! Come on!" says the Vice President. "You are doing more for American pride than a hundred congressmen could do."

"All right, well yeah," Will says. "I'm having a good year. I hope you enjoy the game."

"I will. Hey, Will," the Vice President says, "Me and McConaughey and some of his Hollywood fruitcakes are getting dinner after the game at Rao's. You should join."

"Really?" says Will. His rise to fame has been so meteoric he's still not exactly sure what to do with it. He understands why people want to see him play. But dinner with movies stars? Do they expect him to hit home runs between the antipasto and the fusilli? "Umm, OK," he says. "Thanks."

"Great. Seth will call your agent. Or whoever." The guy in the suit and glasses nods. "See you later then. Don't strike out. I'm from Atlanta, but I'm a Yankee fan tonight!"

That evening, in Yankee stadium, before fifty thousand fans including the Vice President of the United States, the first place Yankees are playing the second place Boston Red Sox. It is 1-0 due to Will's earlier leadoff home run. Will steps into the batter's box for the second time, in the fourth inning. His stats glow on a massive video screen above the stands in center field. He has no singles, no doubles, no triples, no walks or stolen bases. He has three hundred twenty-two home runs. His batting average is 1.0000. There is one out. The bases are loaded.

"'Sup Dobbs?" says the catcher. "Wonder what we should do here."

"Hi, Mike," says Will. "Nice to see you too. That rash clear up?"

"All right, gentlemen," the umpire steps into the smack-talkfest. "Shut up and play baseball."

"We're trying, chief," say the catcher, "but Will here keeps losin' all our balls."

"That's enough, Feeney," the umpire says to the catcher. "Shut up and catch."

"Oh, I will," the catcher says. "Mind if I stretch out a bit?"

Will and the umpire are taken aback as the catcher stands up and sticks his glove out in "intentional walk" position. There is an audible reaction from the fans, and in the Yankee dugout.

"What in the..." Al Gianfranca says to no one in particular.

"Interesting," says Phil Taylor, his mind going through a thousand new future scenarios and contingencies brought by Will Dobbs and his home runs. Tony is watching from the clubhouse.

"Hmm," he says.

Vice President Mahoney is in the stands.

"Well, I'll be a monkey's uncle," he says.

Lester Lowe and Archie Talbot are calling the game.

"Well in a season full of firsts, here's another," Lester says. "The Red Sox are electing to walk in a run, rather than pitch to Will Dobbs."

"I mean, it seems like a dumb move on the surface," Archie says. "No one wants to give up a run, and I think it took the other teams some time to accept this as a fact, but now that we are halfway through the season it's become clear, when Dobbs is the batter, it's walk in one, or give up four."

The pitcher sends the first pitch high and wide. Ball one. Will smiles awkwardly. The crowd boos relentlessly.

Kerry, watching at home while feeding Will Jr. from a bottle, looks concerned.

Ball two. Ball three. Ball four.

"And young Will Dobbs finds himself once again in uncharted territory—on base," says Lester Lowe.

"I hope he remembers how to run," says Archie.

As Will takes a short lead off first base, the next Yankee batter hits the first pitch for a grounder to the shortstop, who tosses to second, beating a somewhat awkwardly sliding Will, and the second basemen throws over to first for the double play. Will gets up and dusts himself off. The crowd is making a confused racket, some are booing, although it's not clear who they are aiming their negativity at, or why.

In the clubhouse after the game, Will's teammates are consoling their slightly dejected slugger.

"You can't hit a dinger every time," catcher Ralph Day says. "That's no fun."

"They'll pitch to you again," says shortstop Richie Pope. "They can't walk you forever."

"But it worked," Will says solemnly. "They won."

"6-5 man, that's not on you," says center fielder Kelvin McDonald. "That's one run. That's on us. We gotta start winning no matter what you do. That's what a team is."

Will brightens up a little.

"Thanks, guys," he says. "I just don't want to let anybody down."

"Hell no, man," says Richie. "We're going to McGinty's. You in?"

"No, thanks," says Will. "I was supposed to have dinner with the Vice President and Matthew McConaughey, but I haven't heard from them."

"He was so good in 'Dallas Buyers Club,'" says Ralph.

Will sighs. "Yeah. I didn't see that one. I saw 'Interstellar.'"

"Now that was one weird ass flick," says Kelvin.

"Seriously," Richie says. "Like, time and space, like, folded or something."

They all drift off in thought for a moment.

"I think I just want to go home to my boy," Will says. "Maybe tomorrow."

"All right," says Kelvin, "If you see McConaughey, tell him that space shit was crazy."

The players file out, leaving Will alone in the clubhouse. He sits for a few minutes, not sure what to do. He checks his phone for any word from the Vice President and sees none. Tony enters the room with a bucket and broom.

"Oh, hey Will," he says. "Thought it was empty."

"No, it's OK, come on in."

Tony notices Will's glum mood.

"You OK?" he asks.

"Not really," Will answers.

Tony sits on a bench near Will and says, "What is it? You've got a beautiful wife, a beautiful baby boy, you get to play baseball for a living. A pretty good one at that."

Tony's calm words have the opposite effect. Will turns to him and blurts out, "Why doesn't anyone understand? It's not about the money, the fame, it's not even about the game. Yes, I have a beautiful wife and son, but the one thing that I want more than anything, I can't have. You wouldn't understand that!"

Tony turns his eyes from Will down to his prosthetic leg. He subtly taps it a few times.

Message received. Will says, "I'm sorry, Tony. I didn't mean to yell at you. I'm just mad. Not at you, of course. Everything else."

"That's all right," Tony says, still looking down. "Life threw you a big curveball tonight."

"More like a big stupid intentional walk."

"Well, yes, technically speaking." Tony says. "Three of 'em."

Will takes a long moment contemplating his future and all the curveballs that have been thrown at him since that one errant fastball changed the course of his life a little over a year ago. "I'm looking for something, Tony," he says. "I don't know if I'm ever going to find it. It's like a hole in my heart that I need to fill. And all the money and fame and glory aren't going to fill it."

"I understand how you feel," Tony says. He looks up, not at Will, but across the spacious clubhouse. He doesn't see lockers or benches or uniforms or cleats. He's looking at another place, another time. A better time. "I got one of those too," he says.

Will was unaware that Tony even had moods. He was sort of a reliable piece of equipment around the clubhouse. Always there, doing his job perfectly every day, always good for a quick easy chat about baseball. You never had to put in any effort, Tony did all the work. But now, Will could see the tears welling in Tony's eyes and he felt guilty. Tony was hurting. Will never really saw that, until now. When Tony realizes that he is losing control of his emotions in front of a player, the best one that ever lived no less, he's embarrassed and a little worried.

"Please don't tell…" he says quietly. "I'm sorry, I'm going to go start in the visitors' locker—"

"Hey," Will says quietly, "It's OK." He pats Tony on the back and looks him in the eye in a way that assures him that not only is Will not going to tell anyone, he's going to sit there until Tony feels better. The two men just sit in silence for a few minutes, looking around the room. Tony wipes a few tears, and takes a few deep breaths.

"Thanks," he says. "I'm fine. Sorry. You were leaving, please don't stay—"

"It's OK," Will says. "I'm pretty sure I've been blown off by the Vice President and Matthew McConaughey. Got nowhere to be."

Tony smiles.

"You want to get a beer?" Will asks.

"Oh. Oh, no. Thanks Will, that's kind of you. You have a family to get home to and I've got work to do. And I actually haven't had a drink in five years."

"Oh wow," Will says, not knowing exactly how to respond. "Sorry about that. Congratulations?"

"No, don't be. Thanks. And you be careful with the booze too, OK. It's cost me. A lot."

Will feels bad for Tony, and he's pretty sure getting into his issues with alcohol right now won't make him feel any better. Will tries to think of anything he can do to make Tony happy.

"Hey," he says as he reaches into his travel bag, fishes around inside, and pulls out a baseball.

"Here," he says, handing the ball to Tony.

"What's this?" Tony asks.

"That's the big one," Will says. "From the All-Star Game."

Tony looks at the ball and sees the official MLB All-Star Game logo imprinted on it. A small scuffed dent is there as well.

"Some maintenance guys found it behind a bunch of pipes in the rafters and got it to me," Will says. "Well, after I got him Yanks season tickets."

Tony smiles. "That was a bomb," he says. "I can't take this. It's yours."

"I have plenty," Will says. "This one's yours."

"Really? I mean, I'm sorry about the blubbering. I just had a moment, you know? I'm good. You don't need to do this, Will. I can't."

"OK, fine," Will says. He takes the ball back and says to Tony, "Borrow that Sharpie?"

Tony looks around, a little confused, and Will points to Tony's shirt pocket. There's a black Sharpie sticking out of it.

"Oh. Sure," says Tony, handing it to Will. Will signs the ball and hands it back to Tony, along with the Sharpie.

"It just doubled in value," Will says. "And I wrote your name on it, so you have to take it."

Tony looks at the ball. Will has written "Hey Tony, This Bomb's 4 U! -Will Dobbs" on it. Tony tries to smile. "I don't know what to say."

"You don't have to say anything," Will says. "Your phone have a camera in it?"

Tony fumbles around and pulls out an old flip style phone from his pocket.

"I think so. I just never—"

"Lemme see," Will says as Tony hands him the phone.

"That there's the call button," Tony says. "And I think you can write a text with that one…"

Will beeps a few buttons, finds the camera after a moment, and says, "OK, here we go. Get over here, Tony. Hold that thing up."

Tony sits next to Will, who puts one arm around him and extends the phone in the other to take a selfie with Tony, and the ball.

"Smile," Will says, and Tony does. Will snaps the picture and takes a look. "Good," he says. "Lotta fakes out there. Now you have proof yours is the real deal. I will not be offended if you sell it. I hear they are getting twenty grand on eBay."

Will hands the phone back to Tony and gets up to leave.

"Bye, Will. Thank you," Tony says.

"You got it."

As Will leaves, Tony opens his phone and looks at the picture of Will and himself.

"eBay, my ass," he says, tucking the phone back into his pocket.

CHAPTER 19

Will and Kerry are in the kitchen on a summer Sunday morning. Kerry is reading The Post and drinking coffee, while Will is unsuccessfully trying to feed baby Will in his high chair. Will Jr. is well coated in whatever is supposed to be going into his mouth.

"Mama. Mama! Look at me!" Will says. "I'm eating like a big boy. Mama. Mama!"

"What?" Kerry says looking up from the paper. "Oh, sorry. Yes, that's a big boy. Careful, you might get some in his mouth."

"Oh no!" says Will. "He just likes to wear a little. Open. Show Mama. Open… Mama!"

Will Jr. opens, accepts, then rejects the yellowish food all over the table, and his father.

"Good boy," says Will and looks at Kerry, who is not watching the heroic display of baby food re-distribution. She is buried in the paper again. "Kerry?"

"Sorry, babe, you know the reporter that was going after you?"

"Greenwald? Yes."

"He's at it again."

"Still with the drugs?"

"No, he's done with that."

"What's his problem now?" Will says, clumsily shoving a spoonful into Will Jr.'s cheek/eye socket area. "Oops, sorry buddy."

"He's calling to have you banned."

Will stops feeding mid-spoonful. "Banned?! Why? Because I'm good?"

"He's saying it's not fair for you to play. He's saying you're ruining the game. He says you are some sort of biological freak that shouldn't be allowed to play."

"What am I, Frankenstein? Jesus, it's not my fault I can hit every pitch for a home run."

Kerry flips back through pages of the obviously quite lengthy article.

"He says that, right… here: 'Dobbs' superhuman ability is not his fault, per se, but that's not the issue. The issue is the integrity of the game.'"

"That's ridiculous," Will says and continues to feed baby Will.

"Is it?"

Will stops feeding again and stares at Kerry. "What are you saying, Ker? I'm doing something wrong?"

"No, Will. I, and Stan Greenwald, aren't accusing you of doing anything wrong. But you have to admit, baseball never intended for you to happen. It's not really equipped to handle you."

"Fine. It's not. So what do you want me to do, Ker? Play worse? Quit? Fine, I'll just quit. I'll go work in a Modell's or something."

"Will, don't overreact. I just want you to be prepared. While everyone is sky high on Will Dobbs right now, that could change."

"Change to what, Ker? Baseball is baseball. It's survived wars, strikes, steroids, depressions. It will survive me."

"I don't know, Will. Greenwald is saying that baseball will need to evolve and survive somehow, if you keep playing. It might be a tough transition, that's all."

"If?! Are you siding with Greenwald?" Will is starting to get annoyed. As is Kerry.

"This isn't about sides, Will. I'm just trying to help you."

"Telling me my future in baseball is in jeopardy? That's helping?"

"I didn't say that."

"Yeah, you kinda did, Ker."

"I'm saying that Stan makes a valid point. Baseball is going to survive no matter what. There's too much at stake for it not to. You need to figure out how to as well. How to stay a part of it."

"OK, well, you are not helping." Will gets up from the table. "I have to get ready."

"Will, you didn't finish breakfast," Kerry says. "Neither did your son."

CHAPTER 20

The first place New York Yankees are playing the last place Tampa Bay Devil Rays. They are winning, 6-0. It's the eighth inning. There is no one on base. Will Dobbs steps up to the plate.

"Well, it's been a strange mixed bag for Dobbs tonight," game announcer Lester Lowe says. "Jeffries intentionally walked him twice. Dunham felt lucky and tried to pitch to him, that resulted in three runs for New York in the sixth. Now Camacho is in, and he's never faced Dobbs."

"And Camacho is not one to shy away from a hot hitter," says commentator Archie Talbot. "Let's see what he does."

As the often unhittable reliever Alfonso Camacho sets, the catcher stays down in a standard crouch behind the plate. The crowd cheers loudly, as they've come to do on the rarer and rarer occasions when Will Dobbs is actually pitched to. Camacho winds and delivers. The pitch goes so far high and behind Will he doesn't even think about swinging at it. The crowd starts booing and shouting. Will gives Camacho a look. Camacho returns it. The catcher stands up. The umpire steps in. Players from each bench stand up.

"OK, easy fellas," says the umpire. "Calm down. Camacho, that's a warning! One more like that and you're gone!"

"It slipped," says Camacho. "I'm sorry."

Once all the players have calmed and returned to their proper positions, Camacho sets again. As he does, the catcher stands up in "intentional walk" position.

"What in the..?" Phil Taylor mutters in the dugout.

"Man, they are trying anything," Al Gianfranca, standing next to him, answers.

"Can't really blame them," says Phil.

Will looks toward Al. Al gives him the "stay calm" hand gesture. Camacho sets and delivers. Instead of a pitchout, it's a ninety-five-mile-per-hour fastball, and it's headed straight for Will. Will barely ducks out of the way as he lands in a heap in the dirt. The crowd gasps and starts yelling angrily. The catcher can't hold Will back as he races toward Camacho. Both benches clear instantaneously and converge in a mass of swinging, wrestling humanity, on and around the pitcher's mound.

Stan Greenwald is watching from the press box amongst the reporters. He'd written about Will's hero days being numbered, and now he was watching it happen. There was no place in baseball for perfection. Perfection was boring.

Perfection didn't fill the seats. A reporter whispers to him, "Oh God, what is happening?"

Stan stares emotionless at the melee on the field. "Evolution," he says.

Later that night, Will is sitting at a local bar, somewhere between Yankee Stadium and his Westchester home, sipping a bourbon with one hand and holding an ice pack over a swollen right eye with the other. Al Gianfranca is with him, looking intently at his glass of beer.

"I almost died from getting beaned once, Al," Will says between sips. "I can't let guys get away with that stuff."

"I know," Al says, "I hear ya, kid. You gotta protect yourse—" Al cuts off mid-sentence, suddenly looking around the bar at the multitudes of well-groomed, fashionably-dressed men. "Is this a gay bar?!" he asks, somewhat shocked.

Will smiles. "Yeah. It's the only place I get left alone. I love it."

"Well, Jesus Christ kid, ya coulda given me a little warning. I was having flashbacks to Vegas 1998 when I saw Barbra Streisand at Caesars. I woulda worn nicer shoes."

Will smiles and calls to the bartender, "Hector! Two more!"

"Take it easy kid," Al says. "We got a big one tomorrow."

"Does it really matter, Al? They pitch to me, I knock it out; they don't, I walk. Doesn't matter how many drinks I have."

Will downs his drink. Al looks a bit concerned.

"What's up, kid?" he asks. "You got a lot of good stuff going on in your life right now. You shouldn't be drinking bourbon in a gay bar in Riverdale with an old, straight man."

Hector the bartender puts a bourbon and a beer in front of them.

"Thanks, Hector," Will says and takes a sip. "Al, am I the greatest hitter that ever played baseball?"

Al thinks for a minute. He knows the answer, he's just trying to figure out how to frame it for his young, fragile superstar. "Well, kid, there was Ruth, Williams, Mantle—"

"Al?" Will stops Al mid-thought.

"Well, yes kid, after your one season, you are. What's the point?"

"I'm the best there ever was. And I was never a jerk to anyone. What do I get? Fans bugging me everywhere I go, haters booing me, pitchers trying to kill me, and the press wants to ban me."

Al's first reaction is to call Will a spoiled brat and smack him in the head, but the sadness in the young Yankee's eye has some merit. There have been good hitters, great hitters before him, but he is different. Unique. He isn't just good; he is the best anyone could possibly be. When is being the best too good? When does it become bigger than the game, bigger than baseball? This was a young man with his life in front of him. What would that life be? What should it be? Al thought and talked about baseball ninety-nine percent of the time he was awake and dreamed about it most of the time he wasn't. He lost two wives due to this propensity. It's difficult for him to deal with things other than baseball. He looks at the young hyper-talented third baseman sitting next to him, drowning his miseries in Wild Turkey, and realizes that this was one of those things.

"Kid, you know I love you, and hell, I want you to play forever," he says to Will. "But you are in a unique situation. If it's too much, don't let it screw up your life. You can walk away."

"No, Al, I can't."

Al had heard about Will's dad and his original reasons for getting into the game. Man, things didn't turn out like this kid planned, he thinks. Al takes a long sip of beer and says sympathetically, "Kid, I don't think your dad is coming back. Sorry. I'm not trying to get you down. I just think you have enough to worry about without chasing gho— I mean… I'm trying to help. Really."

"Well. Yeah." Will says, looking down into the pool of brown bourbon. Al notices Will's knuckles whitening around the glass.

"It's all going to work out," Al says. "Just hang in there."

Will downs the remainder of his drink.

"Well, of course you would say that, Al," he says, looking straight ahead. "Hector! Another!"

Al looks at Will, perturbed, and says to the bartender without taking his eyes off Will, "I'm good, thanks," and then to Will, "What's that supposed to mean, kid?"

"Oh, come on!" Will says, gesturing and air-quoting. "Al Gianfranca, 'Hitting Coach to the Greatest Slugger Ever.' That should get your kids and grandkids through college. Of course you want me to 'hang in there.'"

Now it was Al's turn to down his drink. But unlike for Will, it was not an additional shot of courage, or cure for any pain Al was feeling. It was a sign that this conversation was about to end. His glass empty, he looks Will in the eye.

"I'm gonna forget you said that, kid."

"Why? 'Cuz it's true?"

Al takes a long pause. He looks up at the ceiling, scowls, and takes a deep breath.

"Let me explain something to you, kid. I grew up in what they called Fort Apache in The Bronx, not too far from here. It was so dangerous the cops didn't go there. My dad, unlike yours, really died, when I was three. There was no nice well-to-do couple to come in and save me. My mom raised five of us in a one-bedroom rat hole. We had nothing, kid. My little brother died of some disease only the rich people's doctors could cure when he was nine. There were a lot of tears, kid. Lot of tears and a lot of roaches. Roaches and friggin' rats. But you know what we did have? We had a black and white TV that someone left out on the curb, and if we got the wire hanger on top of it bent and pointed in the perfect direction and smacked it in just the right spot on the left side, and if the weather was just right, we could watch the Yankees play. Me and my brothers and sisters would get around the TV on game night, sometimes with empty stomachs, and wait for Mantle to get up to bat. If he hit one out, we turned down the sound and listened for the real cheers from the Stadium out the kitchen window. We forgot how hungry and poor we were, just for a moment. I'll never forget that feeling kid, it's the only good memory I have from that time. It was magic. And you know what? I've seen a lot of good players, hundreds, but I never got that same feeling again until I saw you hit, kid. So if you think I'm sitting here trying to help you get through this shit storm that has formed around you because of money, you ain't paying attention kid."

Al grabs his coat, angrily slaps a twenty on the bar, and leaves.

Will sits quietly, and downs his drink.

"Hector!" he yells.

CHAPTER 21

It's the bottom of the ninth inning. The Yanks are down 5-4 to the Blue Jays. Will is at bat. He's looking a little bleary-eyed. Or bored. Another intentional walk. There are some boos from the less than capacity crowd as Will heads to first. Stan Greenwald is in the press box, chatting with another reporter.

"Great article on Dobbs," says the reporter.

"Oh yeah. Thanks."

"Any movement on the ban?" he asks Stan.

"Not really. I don't think it's an issue anymore."

"Really? I thought you said he should be gone. You aren't pushing for a ban anymore?"

Will takes a small lead off first and the Yankee batter hits one deep to right field. Will slips back to the bag and prepares to tag up. The right fielder catches the ball and heaves it to second as Will scrambles, stumbles, and dives to beat the throw. He doesn't. The crowd boos. Will gets up and shoves the second baseman, who shoves him back. Again, both benches clear and umpires and coaches grapple with players to quell the melee. Booing fans begin to get up and head for the exits, more interested in beating New York City traffic than seeing how the fight, or game, end. Stan gives a knowing glance to his colleague.

"I don't think I have to," he says.

Will arrives home, late, disheveled, with a cut over one eye. Kerry is waiting for him.

"Will, this has to stop," she says.

"What, Kerry? What exactly has to stop?"

"Keep your voice down. The fighting! The fines! You getting hurt! Suspended! How is this a good thing for anyone?!"

"Just… just stop watching the games, Ker, OK?"

"I will not," she says. "It's the only way I know what's really going on with my husband."

"Kerry, these guys are all out to get me. I have to defend myself. I have enough money to pay any fine a thousand times over. What do you want from me?"

Kerry looks at Will with a new kind of surprise.

"Are you drunk?!" she says in an angry whisper.

"I had one drink after the game."

"One? Really? That's what you said this morning after I heard you puking in the middle of the night, Will."

"I had a few drinks. I have a driver. What are you going to do, ground me?"

"This isn't about what I will or won't or can or can't do to you, Will. It's about what you are doing to yourself. To your family. What are you doing exactly, Will? Is this part of your big plan? Go into a coma, come out, become the best baseball player ever, then try to find your father in every bar in New York City?!"

Will is simmering, but stays calm. "No, Kerry. That is not the plan."

"I don't like this. Not at all, Will."

"What don't you like, Ker? The big house? The nice car? The friggin' boulders I put on your fingers? What's got you so down, babe?"

Kerry feels the conversation devolving into where it has gone far too often lately, anger and insults.

"I think we should talk about this tomorrow."

"I am open to any suggestions you have, Kerry. I'm the best ever. No one can ever get me out. Ever." Will is slurring and getting louder and angrier.

"Keep. Your voice. Down." Kerry says.

"But these wussies won't pitch to me!" Will is yelling now. "Damn cowards, they are screwing up my life. Not me! And now you are pissed at me?! I don't need this, Kerry. I really don't!"

Will Jr. begins to cry from his upstairs bedroom. Will and Kerry look toward the sound.

"Oh great," Kerry says. "Perfect."

Will takes a step toward the stairs. "I'll go—"

"NO!" Kerry says with an up till now unseen resolve in her voice. Will, startled, stops in his tracks.

"You do not go near our child like this. I will go take care of him. You take care of yourself."

Kerry steps past Will and heads upstairs. Will walks slowly into the dark kitchen, expressionless. He stands in the middle of the room, stares at the refrigerator for a moment, then punches it, hard, resulting in a dented appliance, and a bloodied knuckle.

CHAPTER 22

Will hurriedly enters the Yankee clubhouse to find the rest of the players already dressed and ready for the day's game. Veteran ace Zach Hanson sees Will enter in a tardy pseudo-panic.

"Hey, Wonderboy," he says jokingly. "Lose the keys to the Wondermobile?"

A wave of friendly snickers ripples through the team, as the guys head toward the door of the tunnel that leads to the diamond. Will isn't snickering. His head is pounding from an unusually brutal hangover. His brain hurts and he's angry. Angry at his team, and the world, and himself.

"Up yours, Hanson," he says. "Lucky I showed up at all the way you been pitching."

All snickering stops.

"Jesus Christ, Dobbs," Hanson says putting his hands up innocently. "I was just kidding. Is there something you want to talk about?"

The rest of the team stops to see how this unorthodox pitcher-batter duel plays out. There had been tension between these two superstars at the start of the season, which eventually turned to a mutual respect for each other's talents as they spearheaded the Yankees charge to the playoffs. The early animosity seems to have returned of late.

"Just not in the mood for your garbage today, OK, Zach?" Will grumbles, struggling with his spikes.

"All right there, Will, understood. I'm done giving you any." He thinks for a moment before he adds, "Maybe we're all getting a little tired of yours."

The team doesn't move a collective muscle. This is a moment they have been waiting for. They just didn't know exactly how or when it would arrive, or how or when it would end. Will abandons his uncooperative spikes and lashes out at the Yankee ace.

"My what, Hanson?! My one-thousand average? My four hundred home runs? My getting us to the playoffs?" He notices the rest of the team looking and listening, and catches their unsympathetic vibe. "What are you all tired of, exactly, huh?!" Will is getting agitated, still trying to get dressed. Hanson answers for the team.

"No one's saying you aren't a good player, a great player, Dobbs, that's obvious," Hanson says. "But Richie's on the DL now with a sprained wrist, Sal's out indefinitely with a scratched cornea, and Rico's still out with the broken thumb. All from the past coupla fights, Will. It's a lot of fighting and not a lot of baseball going on lately, ya know? If we wanted to fight like this we'da taken up hockey."

Some of the players nod in agreement.

"When your slugger gets thrown at, you defend him, right?" Will asks them all. "That's part of the game, right?"

"No one threw at you last night, Dobbs," Hanson says. "You got thrown out at second."

"Gamson tried to hit me with his glove!! And spike me! You didn't see that?!"

Hanson suddenly feels less like a Major League pitcher and more like he does when his eight-year-old son throws a tantrum about eating his broccoli.

"OK, Dobbs, that's cool," he says. "I'm just saying. Maybe dial it all back, a little."

"I'm not dialing anything back, Hanson!" Will yells at him. "You're lucky I'm here. You are all lucky I'm on this team! I'm bringing you to the World Series. I'm your endorsement deals, your Porsches, your Tahitian vacations with your wives or girlfriends! I'm buying your boats and your beach houses. So you got a little beat up, it's your job. Tough! Suck it up!"

Some on the team look as if they want to say something to him. Some look like they'd like to do more than talk. Hanson surreptitiously holds out a reassuring hand towards the team. He speaks before things escalate.

"OK, Will. Message received," he says. "Let's have a good game, fellas."

Will is still frantically struggling to get ready for the start of the game. He could use a hand, but when he looks up, there's no one in the clubhouse but him.

"Here we are on a beautiful, sunny September afternoon in the Bronx, getting ready to watch the New York Yankees try to officially clinch a playoff berth against the Orioles," Lester Lowe announces to the millions of viewers tuning in around the world. The dignified timbre of his deep baritone remains, while the enthusiasm and joy in the delivery seems to have waned.

"You say 'officially' because as we all know, with Will Dobbs on the team, even walking almost every at bat, the Yanks have a thirteen-game lead on the second place Red Sox," Archie Talbot adds. "It's kind of a foregone conclusion."

"Which would explain some of the empty seats…"

At this point a producer with a headset on jumps up and gives a silent "Cut that!! No!! No!!" hand signaled sign to Lester, who shrugs at him dismissively.

"OK," Lester continues. "And speaking of Will Dobbs, here he is, batting lead-off again tonight."

"It's been a year of broken records for Dobbs this season," Archie says. "Most home runs, obviously. Also, most walks, and most fines for a single player in a season—4.6 million dollars."

"Oh, OK hold on!" Lester chimes in with feigned enthusiasm, "Eight, nine, ten, OK! He just earned that 4.6 mill! OK, here we go. Pitcher sets… and in a shocking maneuver, they're gonna walk him, Arch!"

The producer facepalms.

Nate Felder, a 6-foot 6-inch, 280-lb. Nebraska farm boy with a sniper rifle for a right arm, sets and nods to the catcher, Dylan Munsey, who is standing in "intentional walk" position. The pitcher winds and tosses it—behind Will. The catcher is prepared for the inevitable response. He ignores the wild pitch and steps in to restrain an infuriated Will. The crowd boos, less in anger at the pitcher than at seeing this all-too-familiar scenario play out once again.

"Easy, Wonderboy," Munsey says.

"Easy, Dobbs," the umpire says half-heartedly. "Felder, that's a warning," he says, threatening to toss the pitcher after his one pitch outing. The Orioles already have another starter warmed up and standing at the bullpen exit gate. The umpires have had about enough of the Dobbs-fueled fighting, and there's not much they can do outside of avoiding getting hurt themselves. Baseball has become a game full of new codes, untested strategies and unwritten rules, that all seem to end with the same result—Will Dobbs' team winning the World Series. Hardly seems worth getting injured over. Tonight's field boss stays a safe distance from the impending fracas.

"Damn you, Munsey!" Will yells at the catcher, over the crowd's boos. "What the hell was that?!"

"It slipped," says Munsey, calmly using his squat catcher-shaped body to physically block Will from getting at the pitcher. "He's sorry."

This exchange just makes Will angrier, and he begins screaming in Munsey's face, and over his shoulder at Felder. After Will bumps him one too many times, Munsey bear hugs him and lifts him in the air, hauling the much smaller Will away from the pitcher like a rag doll. The crowd is booing relentlessly. The catcher heads toward the Yankee dugout with a kicking, struggling Will locked in his solid grip.

"This is bull!" screams Will. "You suck, Felder! We're gonna kill you, Felder!! We're gonna kill you guys!! We're gonna beat the piss out of you!!"

"We?!" Felder yells from the mound, holding out his hands in questioning fashion.

Will stops thrashing and yelling and looks around. To his horror, he realizes he's alone. No one has left the bench, from either team. The catcher Munsey roughly deposits Will in the dirt warning track in front of the Yankee dugout.

"I believe this belongs to you," he says to the Yankees, as he shakes his head, turns and walks calmly back toward home plate.

Will looks into the dugout. He sees the coaches and managers making no moves to help him. Many have their arms crossed, waiting. Just waiting. He sees Al turn and walk away into the depths of the dugout. He sees manager Phil scribbling something in a playbook. He sees Zach Hanson spit a disdainful wad of chew on the ground and give a "toldja so" look in his direction. The crowd has stopped booing. Will hears a sound that shakes him to the core. They are laughing. Presumably, at him.

Felder walks up to Will, towering over him. Will gets to his feet.

"Looks like it's just me and you, Wonderboy," he says, smiling. "Wanna give it a go?"

"Dobbs," says the umpire, hustling over. "I would strongly suggest for a large number of reasons that you do not give it a go."

Will is crazed with disbelief and embarrassment, as well as a sizable hangover.

"I'm not!" he says to the umpire, nearly in tears. He looks wildly at Felder. "Pitch, you jackass!"

Felder really wants to clobber Will, but as he looks at him, standing there, dirty and shaken, looking more like one of the scared kids he used to harass on the playgrounds and ballfields of his youth than the best hitter that ever was, he shakes his head and returns to the mound. Will dusts himself off and heads back to the batter's box. Munsey and the umpire return to their respective places. The crowd is booing, hissing and laughing. Will looks sad and broken.

"OK," says the umpire. "Everybody ready to play some baseball?"

"Yeah, I'm ready," Will says, looking as if he might cry.

The pitcher sets and nods to the catcher, who stands up in "intentional walk" position. The pitcher tosses high and wide, and the catcher sidesteps to collect it.

"Ball two!" bellows the umpire.

The crowd boos mercilessly. Surrounded by fifty thousand hometown fans and the team he is bringing to the World Series, Will Dobbs, the greatest baseball player that ever lived, feels incredibly alone.

CHAPTER 23

It's a cold November evening in the Bronx. Will sits at a large conference room table, deep in the corporate sector of the Yankee Stadium complex. His agent, manager, and lawyer are with him. Ted Beasley, the team owner, has called a meeting. He enters with a team of two business managers and three lawyers.

"Yeesh," Will says looking at them. "All for me?"

Ted looks at him, puts his briefcase on the table, and sits. "How are you, Will?" he asks.

"Still recovering, you know," Will answers, smiling. "Quite a party they throw for you when you win the World Series."

"Yes, it was," says Ted, half-smiling.

"So, what's up?" Will asks. "You need me to do some stuff in the off-season, hug babies, shake hands, that kinda—"

"We've gotta let you go, Will," Ted interrupts.

"What did you say?" Will asks.

"We're letting you go," Ted says calmly. "You're going to be off the team."

Will lets out a dismissive laugh. "You're joking, right? Is this one of those stupid 'YES Network' station promos?" He looks around the room. "Where are the cameras?"

"I'm sorry, Will," Ted says. "I know how much being a Yankee meant to you."

Will has now heard, and understands what his boss initially said. He can't believe it's actually true. This must be some bizarre negotiating technique the suits are pulling. Why hadn't his agent warned him? He looks to his agent, who is looking at his feet, out the window, anywhere but at Will. His manager is intensely trying to remove a nonexistent piece of lint from his jacket sleeve. Since neither of them is apparently going to, Will has no choice but to talk.

"But, you can't," Will says. "I mean. I just won it all. I just… we just won!"

"We did, yes," says Ted. "To a lot of empty seats, Will. And as far as TV, it was the lowest rated World Series ever."

Will's mood changes from defiant to defensive as the gravity of the situation begins to envelope him.

"But, but that's not my fault. I mean, everybody loved me at the beginning of the season. We got huge ratings then, right? Doesn't that mean anything? I can still hit home runs. It's not my fault they stopped watching. Not my fault they stopped pitching to me."

"Nobody is blaming you, Will," says Ted, causing one of the Yankee lawyers to hold up his hand and lean in to whisper something in Ted's ear. "Ah shut up, Barry!" Ted yells at him. The affronted attorney throws up his hands and settles back in his chair.

"The game's changed, Will," Ted says. "You came in and changed it. And now, I'm up to my eyeballs in lawsuits from season ticket holders, cable companies, I've got sponsors and affiliates scrambling to get out of their deals… It's a huge mess. We're projecting attendance and viewership numbers that could literally bankrupt the Yankees. We can't go into another season with the entire business of baseball on thin ice. I know you didn't intend for any of this to happen, or for it to end this way. I'm sorry."

Will is angry, but still in disbelief. He is trying to figure out the exact game being played here. He understands the conundrum the Yankees and Major League baseball are in, but is quite certain that it's their problem, not his.

"End?" he says in defiant confusion. "With all due respect, Ted, I'm not sure what's going on here, but nothing is ending for me. I have a seven-year contract."

He looks at his agent and manager, who are now fiddling with their phones and scribbling on papers. One of the Yankee lawyers slides a sheet of paper to Will.

"What's this?" Will asks.

"Part of your contract," Ted says. "The important stuff's highlighted."

Will reads the highlighted section aloud. "Player shall not engage in behavior gravely detrimental to the organization. Failure to do so will be grounds for immediate termination." He looks at his lawyer. "When did this get added in?" he asks angrily.

"It didn't," his lawyer answers. "It's standard in every player's contract."

Will feels stupid for a moment and looks down at the papers, thinking he should have actually read them before signing them. But then he remembers, that's what he pays the lawyers to do.

He looks up from the contract and turns quickly to his lawyer. "You knew this was happening today," he says to him accusingly. "Get ready to defend yourself in court, Myles."

Will's lawyer looks at him, "Now hold on, Will," he says. "Yes. Ted's guys approached us about this, several weeks ago, actually. We negotiated, and Ted agreed to let you play in the Series, even enjoy the parade and parties and all. We tried to keep you out of the discussion. As far as the termination, there's not much I can do, Will. While this is uncharted territory in many regards, the detrimental behavior language in the contract is pretty clear."

"Detrimental behavior?!" Will yells, turning back to Ted. "I just got you another goddamn World Series!"

"There's the team, and then there's the Yankees organization, Will," Ted explains. "Your skill has gotten the team another championship. But your behavior cost the Yankees organization a ton of money and created endless PR nightmares and legal quagmires that frankly, we are unsure how to get ourselves out of. Combined with your salary, low ticket sales, and advertisers fleeing, we just can't afford to keep you around."

Will thinks about the thousands of fans screaming his name back in the spring, and the same ones booing and laughing in the fall, and it starts to dawn on him that this might not be a game.

"I am getting fired and losing half a billion dollars because I'm too good?!" Will asks. "If I struck out every time you would still have to pay me to sit on the bench, but because I'm so good the game can't handle it, I'm unemployed?!"

"The team has written up a generous severance package," says Ted quickly, attempting to circumvent this moral and financial ambiguity. "I think you will find it more than satisfactory."

"Take your severance package and stick it up your ass, Ted," Will says angrily. "I'll be signed by another team within the hour. Tell him, Mike."

Mike Stern, Will's agent, shakes his head.

"Sorry, Will," he says. "We checked. There was no interest. It's not just the Yankees bottom line that's in trouble. Every fan knows what's going to happen to their team when you are playing against them. They ain't gonna win. So, they ain't gonna watch."

"No one wants me, even though I would bring them to the World Series," Will says.

"Like we said, son," Ted says. "Uncharted territory."

Will's demeanor changes from angry and defiant, to sad and hopeless.

"But… I mean. I can't," he says. "I have to… this is it? It can't be."

"I'm sorry, Will. We had no choice," Ted says. "I'm afraid this is it."

Will sits silently in his chair, numb. "OK," he says.

"There's a release going out tomorrow morning," Ted tells Will.

"OK," says Will again, still in shock.

"OK, then," Ted says as he collects his briefcase. "Well, unless anyone has any questions, I guess we're done here." He gets up to shake Will's hand.

"Will, it's been, well, an unforgettable adventure to say the least. I hope we can work together again someday."

Will takes Ted's hand and is reluctant to let go. Still holding it, he asks weakly, "How?"

"Well, I don't know, son. Who knew a kid from south of Boston would come out of a coma the best baseball player who ever lived? Life's full of curve balls. Take care, Will. Good luck to you." He lets Will's hand go, and walks out of the room.

A few hours later, Tony walks into the Yankee clubhouse with some hand tools in a canvas bag. He sees a notice taped to the door. It reads:

LOCKER RE-ASSIGNMENTS FOR 2019:

EAMONS

GASPARI

DOBBS

"Oh, no," he says, standing there, not wanting to believe it.

As he walks toward the players' lockers, he sees someone stretched out, asleep on the floor at the far end of the room. He approaches warily. He recognizes Will, in the same clothes that he wore to the earlier meeting, asleep in front of his locker. His head rests on a small duffel bag, filled with his personal belongings. Tony looks at him for a moment and decides the locker reassignment task can wait till morning. He grabs a training blanket from a shelf, and drapes it over the young former slugger, gently bringing it up under his chin. He looks down at Will for a long time, just watching him sleeping. Tony smiles through his sadness.

"Sweet dreams," he says, touching Will on the shoulder. He walks to the door, turns out the light, and leaves.

Al Gianfranca is woken up by the shrill ring of the phone. It's 7:30AM. He clumsily grabs the phone from its bedside cradle and presses the answer button.

"Somebody better be dead," he says groggily. Al's perpetual grumpiness increases exponentially if he's required to do anything before 8AM.

"Al? Hi, it's Kerry Dobbs."

"Oh, hi, Mrs. Dobbs," Al says apologetically, shaking off the cobwebs. "Sorry, I'm just getting up. Everything OK?"

"I'm not sure. Will didn't come home last night after his meeting with Ted and the agents, and he's not answering his cell. I was wondering if you had any idea where he might be."

"Ah man," Al says. "I guess he took it hard."

"Took what hard?" Kerry asks.

Al sits up and rubs his eyes, realizing. "You didn't hear?"

"Hear what, Al? Is he OK?"

"The Yanks let him go, Mrs. Dobbs."

There's a small gasp from Kerry's end of the line. "Oh no. No, I didn't hear. Oh, gosh. No."

"I have no idea where he is Ms. Dobbs. But I'm sure he's fine."

"I'm worried, Al. He hasn't been himself lately at all. There's been so much stress. Now this."

Al thinks for a minute. He was pretty sure Will was OK, but he, like Kerry, was starting to think about how fragile and confused the young ball player had been recently, and wondering how this latest unexpected event might affect him. "Listen," he says, "Give him some time. He'll turn up. OK?"

"OK. Let me know if you hear anything before then."

"Of course," Al says. "Hang in there."

Kerry hangs up the phone, scoops Will Jr. out of his ExerSaucer contraption and puts him in his crib for a mid-morning nap. She stretches out on a couch in the living room. The yearlong emotional roller coaster she's been on, combined with suddenly being hit with the prospect of post-baseball life with Will, has drained her. She closes her eyes, and sleeps.

A knock on the door awakens Kerry. She rubs her eyes, goes to the door and opens it. Will is standing there. Not drunk, or angry, but quiet and sad. Kerry sees a different kind of sadness in her husband, not the kind that comes from unsuccessfully trying to assign blame for your life's unexpected misfortunes on others, but the kind that comes from realizing you have a deep hole to climb out of. A hole you partially dug yourself. He's not the same man he was a few months ago, but he looks like he might now be prepared to be a man again. Not necessarily a baseball player, but a father, and a man.

"Can I come in?" he asks meekly.

Kerry holds her arms out to him. Will collapses into them, crying like she's never heard him cry before.

CHAPTER 24

Will rolls around on his bed, wrestling with Will Jr., who has grown a lot since baseball season ended four months ago. Will tosses him in the air and tickles him, sending the little guy into fits of laughter. After a cold winter of reflection and realization, Will has found love and joy in his son and his family.

Baseball fans read dozens of accounts and analyses of the end Will's baseball career. Many were furious, many glad to have witnessed one of the greatest baseball stories begin and end before their eyes. Many were relieved that next season would bring less magic, but more normalcy.

Will lays on his back and holds Will Jr. aloft in "flying baby" position, eliciting squeals of delight from his son.

"Say, 'I love you, Dada'!"

Will Jr. gurgles and says something vaguely approximating the sentence.

"Yes!" Will says excitedly. "That's it! Dada! Good boy!"

Will Jr.'s eyes move to the framed picture on the nightstand. He reaches a little hand in the direction of the picture. Will talks to him in a quiet voice.

"Yeah. That's Dada's dada. Want to hold it?"

Will puts his son down on the bed. He takes the picture from the nightstand and hands it to Will Jr.

"Now be careful. That's glass."

Will Jr. gurgles and touches the picture.

"Da," he says.

"Yeah. That's right, buddy," says Will.

Will smiles proudly but somberly at his son. Kerry appears in the doorway and smiles at her young men.

"You guys good?" she asks.

"Yeah, we're good," Will says. "He's really talking now. Trying anyway."

"I know, it's amazing," she says. "Hey Will, those charity people called again."

"Oh jeez, really?" Will says, frustrated. "I shouldn't have given the home number. Sorry. They are relentless."

Kerry thinks for a moment, then asks, hesitantly, "Why don't you do it, Will?"

Will looks at her, utterly surprised.

"I already wrote a check," he says gruffly.

Kerry puts her hands on her hips. "That's not what they're calling about and you know it."

"Get paid to hit home runs for a bunch of rich people looking for tax deductions?" he asks. "No thanks. I may be a freak, but I'm not joining the circus."

"Well, that's one way to look at it," Kerry says. "Or, you could think about it as raising a lot of money for a good cause while earning a lot of money for your family." She looks at him sternly. Then smiles righteously.

Will's attitude adjusts as he answers, "We have plenty of money, Kerry."

"Well, yes, right now we do," Kerry says. "But the downside of being really rich and really young is that you have a whole lot of life ahead of you that needs to be paid for. Your severance will run out when you are 29. You, or I, are going to have to do something eventually, if we want the meatball there to go to Yale."

They both look at Will Jr. just as he takes the corner of the metal and glass frame into his mouth and goes for a bite.

"EHHH!" Will and Kerry bark at Will Jr. in parental unison as Will quickly and gently removes the picture from the danger zone, in spite of Will Jr.'s protests.

"We should probably get him to stop eating glass first," Will says. Kerry laughs.

"Think about it?" she asks.

"A hitting show? Ugh," Will says. "I don't know."

"Still beats sitting at a desk every day," Kerry says as she goes to the bed and picks up Will Jr. "C'mere fuzzball, it's lunchtime," she says, hoisting him onto a hip and saying to Will, "Love you."

"Love you too," Will says glumly, still trying to grasp the idea of being the best baseball player who ever lived, and getting the "get a job" talk from your wife. Will takes the framed picture in his hand and looks at it. He looks away from the picture and stares into space for a moment. He's deep in thought as Kerry heads out the bedroom door.

"Ker!" he yells.

"Yes?" she says, returning.

"Next time that charity calls, I'll talk to them."

Kerry smiles. "OK great," she says. "I think it's a good idea."

"Yes," Will says, his thoughts intense, and elsewhere. "Definitely."

CHAPTER 25

A large, enthusiastic crowd fills the metal stands and spills into the surrounding space along the baselines around a suburban ball field on a chilly, not-quite-spring-yet evening. Everyone is listening to a spokeswoman from the "Opportunity Knocks" organization, who's standing near the pitcher's mound behind a microphone. On either side of her is a rag tag team of teenagers, athletes, B and C-list celebrities and corporate honchos, all in softball gear. Will Dobbs is among them, trying to smile.

"As you know," the spokeswoman says, "Opportunity Knocks provides a means for underprivileged students to participate in paid internships at some of the most prestigious companies around the country. Last year we provided one hundred fifty-eight students paid internships at law firms, accounting offices, insurance companies and more." The crowd applauds as she continues, "More important than the pay check, these students all gained invaluable, on-the-job, real world experience, and vital networking connections that will give them access to long-term employment. Today, these students are here to play a little softball with some CEOs of the companies in our network, recording artists, athletes, and film and television stars who were gracious enough to take time out of their busy schedules to be here today."

More applause from the crowd.

"Now, before we start the big game," the spokeswoman continues with an air of dramatic anticipation, "we have a very special treat."

A young assistant wearing a headset approaches Will, tapping him on the arm and gesturing toward home plate. Will makes his way from the group of dignitaries to the batter's box, as a pitcher heads to the mound with a bucket of ten baseballs.

"Will Dobbs is here!" the spokeswoman announces excitedly, and the crowd responds appropriately.

"And Will has agreed to show us some of that magical hitting that made him the most famous baseball player in history, for us, right here, right now! Ten young raffle winners are going home with a special prize tonight. Let's hear it for Will, and retired Yankee pitcher Scott Pender!"

As Will approaches home plate, he reluctantly smiles and waves to the crowd. He looks out to the ten little kids, gloved and ready, standing not in the outfield, but spread out in an arc in the open, empty area beyond the outfield fence. Scott Pender grabs the first ball from the basket and as Will settles in at the plate, music suddenly blasts from the PA system. A pseudo-celebrity who has materialized behind the microphone begins singing R. Kelly's "I Believe I Can Fly." Will, slightly startled, steps out of the batter's box, glances toward the source of the music, breathes deeply, and mutters something under his breath that he's grateful the kids are too far away to hear. He gets set again and nods to the pitcher. The charity event coordinators had asked about having a catcher and Will said it wouldn't be necessary. Pender sets, and delivers. Will casually hits the first ball down the line into right field. It flies over the fence and into the first kid's outstretched glove. He hits the next pitch a little more toward center, also over the fence, to the next awaiting child. Will continues this pattern, hitting the remaining eight balls at nearly identical trajectories, depositing one "home run" after another in each kid's glove, without any of them having to take more than a small step to catch their special prize. The crowd goes crazy with amazement and delight as the tenth kid, standing down the line far beyond the left field fence, catches his ball.

"Will DOBBS!" the spokeswoman yells, but she's barely audible above the screaming fans. Will tips his hat. He feels stupid for what they are clapping about, but man how he's missed that sound.

CHAPTER 26

"Thanks for meeting me, Will. I know this is a bit… strange."

Stan Greenwald and Will have just settled in at a table at a diner in Will's town. Stan had called a number of times and Will finally agreed to chat with his one-time arch nemesis over coffee.

"Well, Stan, you won," Will says. "What can I tell you, I'm out. I'm making the best of it. I've got plenty of time on my hands, so I thought I would take some of it and try to figure out what you are planning on writing about me next. You obviously have something against me, so I figured I'd try to make sure you don't make up anything stupid."

"I have nothing against you," Stan says. "And I've never made up anything about you."

"Yes, you have," Will says.

Stan sips his coffee and patiently waits for an example. Will fumbles with his paper napkin.

"OK, fine. Maybe you haven't technically," Will says. "But it's just the way you wrote about me. I could tell you were out to get me. You wanted to kill my career."

"That is not true," Stan says. "I simply foresaw the imminent death of your career and wrote about it. I didn't cause it, nor did I desire it. I only reported what I saw happening and speculated. And I was right. I completely understand that what I wrote might have been hurtful for you to read, but it absolutely was not personal. I've never even really met you before today."

Will looks at Stan, who shrugs. In the time since his baseball career ended, Will had come to terms with what he'd just heard. Stan was right. Kerry was right. Will was bad for baseball. It wasn't personal. It was simply true.

"Fine," Will says. "So, what are we doing here?"

"I need an article. I'm retiring. I was planning on going out by finding out what you are on, but I might be dead before that happens. I need something else."

Will isn't happy about Stan's continued references to steroids, but he appreciates his honesty.

"I don't think I can help you, Stan. I'm just a suburban dad now. Not much to write about."

"How's retirement treating you?"

"Fine," Will says.

"How do you like being a dad?"

"It's great," Will says.

Stan scowls at Will's highly uninspired answers.

"That it?"

"What do you want me to say, Stan? I'm not a superhero any more. I'm not even a ball player. Kerry wants a dog. Some kid bit Will Jr. at the playground the other day. I have another charity monkeyhump to perform at later today.

This is my life now. I'm learning to like it, but I'm quite sure it's not grand finale article material."

"How's the search for your dad?"

"Nothing new. Sorry."

Stan wanted this to be a peaceful and productive meeting, but he's losing his patience.

"Just tell me what you are on," he says.

"I'm not on anything, Stan. What do you want me to do, pee in this coffee cup for you?"

"How did you do it then?"

"Do you read the papers Stan? The internet? I've said it a million times, I don't friggin' know."

"Come on," Stan says through frustrated laughter. "There's no such thing as magic, kid."

Will takes a sip of coffee and looks Stan in the eye.

"Don't you like magic shows, Stan?"

"No. I hate them," Stan says, staring back. "Once you learn how the tricks are performed you feel stupid and ripped off. It's fraud."

"You know, I just read somewhere that David Copperfield owns his own island in the Bahamas?"

"No kidding? So, what?"

"Well, you are obviously in the minority. People love magic shows. They loved to watch me play."

Stan looks intently at this young slugger.

"What's the trick Will?" he asks. "You're never going back to baseball. Might as well fess up."

"No tricks," Will says smiling. "Just magic."

"An audience at a magic show knows they're going to be tricked," Stan says. "People who watch ball games are there to watch baseball."

"Entertainment is entertainment," Will says and leans back in his chair.

"You tell me how you're doing it and I promise to write it in a way to make you look like a hero. I know you did this all for your dad. I'll write about that. It will be sweet. Maybe it will help find him. Just tell me how you are doing it."

Will thinks for a moment and leans forward and points at Stan.

"You wanted this to end with me getting caught," he says.

"No."

"Yes. Yes. That's it. You said you were right about how this would end up, but you weren't. You were wrong about the steroids. You are about to end your career on a big giant mistake. That's why you are really here, isn't it?"

"No. I just need an article."

"Can't help you there, Stan," Will says getting up from the table.

"Will, come on. Give me something. Come on. I'll make you a hero again."

"I don't want to be a hero again," Will says, "I only want one thing."

Stan thinks for a moment and says, "Your dad."

"Good-bye, Stan," Will says getting up from the table. "Don't call again, unless you find him, because that is the only reason I would ever want to hear from you. Good luck."

CHAPTER 27

Will is about to do his thing at another charity event. This one is bigger than the last, with thousands of fans filling the seats of the Rockland Boulders minor league stadium in Pomona, New York. Will will be performing between the seventh and eighth innings of a pre-season game. Kerry is in the stands with Will's parents and Will Jr. There are local reporters and a television crew. There are ten kids standing in a semi-circle beyond the outfield fence just like the last time. Will raises his hat to the cheering crowd from near home plate. A spokesman for the charity du jour is at the microphone.

"Ladies and gentlemen. Thanks for the warm welcome for Will Dobbs. Now, it is my great honor to introduce our pitcher for the evening. It only makes sense that the man pitching to the best hitter who ever lived, would be the best closing pitcher of all time. A great player, and great friend to LoveWorks International—ladies and gentlemen, Mariano Rivera!!"

Mariano Riviera steps onto the field from the sidelines, to raucous applause. He smiles broadly and waves to the crowd. Will heads over to greet him.

"Mr. Rivera," Will says. "It's great to meet you."

"Likewise, Mr. Dobbs," Mariano says, still smiling brightly. "Please, call me Mo."

"Please, call me Will. OK, Mo, take it easy on me."

"No chance, rookie." Mariano smiles even wider as he trots off to the mound. Will smiles and bounds off toward the batter's box.

"Yes, Dada. That's Dada!" Kerry says and points to a happy yet sensory-overloaded Will Jr.

Mariano takes a ball from the bucket of ten as Will steps into the batter's box. The opening strains of Mariano's daunting entrance song, "Enter Sandman," by Metallica, begins to play through the stadium's PA system. Rivera sets and delivers, the heat turned down significantly from his not too distant MLB days, as Mariano knows how the PR game is played. Watching Will deposit pitch after pitch into the outstretched small-gloved hands beyond the fence, he is enjoying the show as much as the fans. Mariano's smiling, Will is smiling and Kerry, Will Jr. and the fans are as well. The camera crew and reporters are capturing the magical display with footage on tape, and words on paper.

The music has reached its thunderous climax as Mariano is about to pitch the final ball. Will holds his hand up for a quick time out, shakes his head, looks out at the field for a moment, and gives him the nod. Mo delivers.

Will hits a towering fly ball down the left field line. The crowd is on its feet, cheering wildly. The music roars along with the crowd. A small eight-year-old girl stands beyond the outfield fence waiting with a glove too big for her hand and a smile too big for her face. Her smile fades, however, as the ball lands in the grass in left field, on the wrong side of the fence. The crowd goes silent as the ball rolls quickly, as if embarrassed, onto the warning track, and settles under the foam padding at the base of the outfield wall.

The music ends right on cue, the performance it was underscoring having gone quite off-script. The girl beyond the left field fence bursts into tears. Kerry looks stunned, as do Will's parents, the reporters, Mariano Rivera, and Will himself.

"Nice pitch," he says to Mariano Rivera.

"Thanks," Mariano answers awkwardly.

The charity spokesman scrambles to the microphone and flips it on with a squeal of feedback.

"OK! OK, great," he says, launching into damage control mode, "Let's hear it for Mariano Rivera and Will Dobbs. What a wonderful… surprise. Come on, everybody!"

The crowd claps politely. A charity volunteer brings the girl in left field over to collect the ball that didn't quite reach her. Will's eyes find Kerry in the crowd. She shrugs. He shrugs back.

After arriving home and putting Will Jr. to bed, Will and Kerry sit watching the news and eating ice cream. The lead story comes on. A reporter with a very inorganic skin tone emphatically reads from the teleprompter.

"Is the magic gone? Watch what happened at a charity event in Rockland County, New York, earlier this evening."

The television plays footage of Will at bat at the earlier event. Will hits the ball to left, the camera tracking the ball as it settles on the ground. The camera whips back to Will who is just standing and staring. A producer with an earpiece comes into frame, looking at the cameraman.

"Tell me you got that or you're (bleep)ing fired," he says.

The camera tilts up and down, nodding in affirmation.

"You sure you feel OK?" Kerry asks Will.

"I feel totally fine."

"I still want you to go to Dr. Emerson."

"I have an appointment tomorrow morning at ten. I'm fine, Kerry. I was when I was hitting everything over the fences and now I am too. Really."

"Did you..." Kerry pauses, trying to find the appropriate words. "Do you think it... you know... it's gone?"

"I don't know. Not sure." Will says as he digs into his ice cream and looks back at the screen showing the little girl in left field crying, then receiving the most famous non-home run ball in history. "One thing I do know," he says with mouth full of Cookies and Cream and a grin. "That kid's gonna make a fortune."

CHAPTER 28

In the words of the late Yankee catcher and street poet Yogi Berra, it's like déjà vu all over again in the conference room in the corporate offices of the New York Yankees. Will is back, sitting at a large conference table with his agent, manager and lawyer. He's in a warm-up suit this time, however, and looking much healthier and more alert than the last time he was in the room. Yankees manager Phil Taylor and two lawyers are there, along with the team physician and Al Gianfranca. Ted Beasley walks in with PR chief Ken Albrecht and a third lawyer. There is an air of anticipation clouded by a general skepticism in the room.

"Hiya, Will, how's everything? Family good?" Ted is trying to be friendly, but he's suspicious of the goings-on of late, involving the former baseball player known as the Bomber from Beantown.

"Everything's great, Ted," Will says. "I really, really appreciate you taking the time today. I know how, well, weird this all is."

Ted looks at him with something resembling a scowl. Then a vacant smile. He's desperately trying to figure out what this kid is up to, and what his next move will be. Mostly, he's wondering how on earth this meeting is going to play out. He stops thinking and starts talking.

"All right, let's get right down to business," he says. "Doc, what's going on with Dobbs here?"

"Well," says the team doctor, "I examined him before his injury, after it, and now this morning. All the same. He's still a normal, healthy twenty-five-year-old man. I've conferred with his neurologist Dr. Emerson as well. He confirms this assessment."

"Got it. Al?" Ted barks at his pitching coach.

"I took him out on the field this morning after the doc was through with him," Al says gruffly. "I pitched to him. Had Garcia throw a few as well."

"And?" Ted asks anxiously.

"He was hitting like, well, like a normal player," Al says. "Grounders, pop-ups, line drives, fouls, strikes." Ted and everyone are listening intently, not sure how to ask what they want to ask, not knowing who, if anyone, might have the answer. "He hit a few out too," Al adds.

Ted raises an eyebrow at this. "How many?"

Al looks at Will.

"I don't know," Al says. "Seven? Eight?" Will nods in agreement.

"How many pitches?" Ted asks.

"A hundred," Al says.

Everyone pauses for a moment.

"OK, so just for the record," Ted says sternly, "Al, did you see any evidence of that superhuman malarkey, or whatever the hell was giving Dobbs the ability to hit every pitch over the fences last season?"

"Absolutely none, boss," Al says. "In fact, I saw some evidence of him sucking a bit."

"I'm a little rusty, boss," Will says. "I'll get it together."

"Well, don't get it together too much kid, we don't want a repeat of last year," Ted says. "And I haven't made any decision yet." He drums his fingers on the table and suddenly can't get comfortable in his chair. "Damn, this is a tough one. This is just weird."

Ted looks gravely at the young former superstar. Every fiber of his being is telling him to bid the kid good day and get back to running his Yankee empire. His expertise was Major League money, not medical mysteries and magic. But through it all, he actually felt bad for Will. None of this was his fault. Whatever the hell happened to Will when that fastball hit him, he certainly didn't plan or want it. Ted felt bad he had to let him go, and now, what if his powers were really gone? He's not sure how well he'd sleep knowing he'd taken the kid's dreams and career away for no good reason. He was going through all the scenarios in his mind. All messy.

"Are you pulling one on us, Dobbs? I know how much you want to play, find your dad and all that. I'm just trying to run a team here that people want to watch on TV and in the stadium. If you are faking or BSing us, you will get caught and it will not end well for you, I promise you that."

"No, I'm not, Ted," Will says earnestly. "I think it's gone. It feels different up there. It feels like it used to, normal. Hitting is hard again, like it's supposed to be. It's a little scary how hard it is. And listen, I don't want a repeat of what happened last season either, so if I ever feel like it's come back, I promise…"

"Oh, you're going to do more than promise," Ted says harshly. "If I agree to bring you back," he says and then turns to the lawyers at the table, "these pit bulls are going to draw up a contract that says if any of your magic stuff comes back, you are gone. Immediately. Got it? Even if we think it's come back, gone!" He points to the door for emphasis. "You have a hot streak we think is a little too hot—gone! Got it?"

Will nods. "Got it."

Ted adds one more "Got it?" for Will's agent and lawyer, who also nod. Ted breathes, finally getting comfortable in his chair, feeling somewhat in control of an uncontrollable situation. He continues.

"It certainly wouldn't hurt to give the fans something to come out to see this year. We need the revenue. You seem to have your head together, Will, and I liked you before you turned into a huge jackhole last year, but I cannot have that happen again."

"I totally understand," Will says.

"And do you now understand that if anything weird happens, that's it for me, the Yankees, and maybe baseball. And how crazy I am for even considering this?"

"Yes," Will says, starting to see a light of hope.

"Do you want to come back?" Ted asks.

"Yes."

Ted looks at Will's agent. "You guys want to call around other teams? Test the waters at all?"

"Will won't let me," the agent says. "He only wants to be a Yankee."

"Until I say no," Ted says accusingly. "Then you start making calls, right?" The agent shrugs slyly, and Will looks at his feet. "Well, hell if I'm going to let that happen," Ted says as Will looks up with a huge smile on his face.

"Your contract will be incredibly unfair," Ted says. "It will be made very clear that we can get rid of you for just about any reason. You hit too many homers, you're gone; you don't hit enough, gone. You get drunk and piss on a Red Sox fan—again—gone. Understood?"

"Understood," Will says.

"For me to agree to this," Ted continues, "we have to have all control. The contract will favor the Yankees organization, not you, on all matters. Understood?"

"Understood," Will says without hesitation.

Will's agent steps in. "Ted, I gotta let you know. Will has one condition he won't budge on in the contract, before you start drawing it up. It's regarding his salary."

Ted goes from grumpy to enraged in a nanosecond. He stands up and yells, "Are you friggin' kidding me?! This rookie punk screws up the entire game of baseball and—"

"He wants the league minimum," Will's agent interrupts. The silence lingers for a moment.

"Excuse me?" a Yankees lawyer asks, bewildered.

"Union minimum," says the agent. "Not a penny more."

Will nods affirmatively. Ted takes a long moment. He sits back down and looks intently at Will for a long while.

"Do not make me regret this, kid," he says.

Will looks at him, silent, afraid to say anything that could screw up what he thinks is about to happen.

"Welcome back to the Yankees."

CHAPTER 29

Stan Greenwald sits in his darkened office, the late October sun having set long ago. His desk is littered with binders and random piles of paper. There is a computer on it, unused, as Stan still hasn't come to fully trust it. Another weird, wonderful baseball season is coming to an end, the New York Yankees heading to the World Series once again, this time with a "normal" Will Dobbs at third base. The rest of the world seems to have simply accepted that this kid somehow acquired, and then lost, some kind of superpower— but not Stan. He hated not knowing the truth. Even more, he hated not being able to report it. He's loved reporting the world inside baseball to New York and fans around the world, but now, Stan is tired. The months of searching, and not finding out how Will Dobbs obtained superhuman skills with a bat have taken their toll.

He turned in what was hopefully his penultimate article hours ago. He still needed something big to wrap up this bizarre story of the Bomber from Beantown, Will Dobbs, and his career. Stan couldn't go out like this. He, and the story, needed closure. Retired or not, he didn't want to get into another season engrossed in whether Will Dobbs was cheating, faking, lying or for Pete's sake, "magical." He just wanted baseball to be baseball again.

After hitting a wall in the search for Will's birth parents, and not convinced by Will's statements at the diner, Stan shifted his full attention to PEDs. He's sure that whatever Will was on, he's still on it, he's just learned to better hide its effects. He pores through a pile of hand written notes. He takes a sip of his coffee which went cold long ago. He scowls. It's 3AM. "Somebody had to see something," he says to the empty room. "Come on."

He had looked at the usual suspects, the medical and coaching staff, other players, et cetera. He found some unsavory information that would have made for a doozy of a future article, but not a thing on Will. He then looked outside the usual places, even tracking down a lab in Honduras that was rumored to have the latest undetectable stuff. He offered so much money for information that the lab techs started making up lies. One said Will had visited Honduras sometime last year, and when Stan pressed for specifics, it turned out to be at the time Will was in a coma. Another said Will was getting the stuff shipped to his house. Stan staked out his house and saw nothing but diapers and Fresh Direct deliveries.

Stan was currently going through his notes on his interviews of the Yankees' staff. He had spoken to everyone who had contact with Will, from the grounds crew to the ball boys. If Will was using, someone must have seen something.

He goes over the same notes he has dozens of times before, finding nothing new or of interest. Just as his eyelids are about to betray him, he spots something. It's not much, but it's enough to wake him up for a moment longer. He slugs down the remaining dregs of three-hour-old coffee, grabs a small notebook and cross references his find with another.

"Hmm," he says. He stares across the room for a moment, then unburies the keyboard of his computer. He scowls at it, exhales, and starts typing.

"Goo…Gul," he says as he does. He clicks, types in the search box and hits the enter key. He scrolls down the list of results, clicks one and begins reading. His eyes widen. He looks at the papers, and then the screen.

"Son of a… holy cannoli," he says.

CHAPTER 30

"Well, this is quite a climax to one heck of a season," Lester Lowe says from high above fifty thousand screaming fans, to about ten million more watching at home or in sports bars around the world.

"What a short, strange trip it's been, eh, Les?" adds Archie Talbot. "Rookie third basemen Will Dobbs gets beaned, goes into a coma, recovers, returns to baseball the best hitter ever and leads his team to the World Series Championship. He gets fired, loses his home run hitting abilities, gets reinstated and still helps bring his team, the New York Yankees, to the World Series again the following season."

"And here we are, back where it all began, in Yankee stadium," Lester continues. "The Yanks are down 6-4 in this final game seven of the Series. There are two outs, two men on in the bottom of the ninth. I'm not sure I've ever heard a crowd sound like this, Arch."

"Well, here's why. Coming up to bat is Will Dobbs, batting sixth in the lineup tonight," Archie says. "He's had a decent season, all things considered, batting .283 with fourteen home runs."

"A hit keeps the Yanks alive, an out ends their season," Lester says. "And, of course, a homer wins it all."

After Will's second return to baseball in as many years, there were elated fans around the world, but also doubters and naysayers who wondered if Will was masking his superhuman abilities in order to stay in the game. The Yankees making it to the World Series again did nothing to quell their doubts. Amongst the Yankee faithful and thousands of Will Dobbs supporters are a few banners that say, "WILL PUTS THE BS IN DOBBS" and "THERE'S NO LYING IN BASEBALL!" While the magic seemed to have left Will Dobbs and returned to American baseball to a great extent, a new taking of sides was occurring. There was still a divide present—not between favorite teams, or leagues, or players, but between believers and non-believers.

There was more enrapturing this frenzied World Series crowd than just how the game would end, or who would win. The crowd was watching Will Dobbs. Wondering. Was he real? What would happen now, and would it tell them what they wanted to know? Would it strengthen the believers' faith, or fortify the naysayers' arguments against? The pitcher sets…

The crowd is going wild. Amongst the fans, Kerry, Andrew and Stephanie Dobbs sit and watch, white knuckles clutching armrests or anything else in their grasping vicinity. Sitting behind the glass of the VIP booth, Andrew has his glove on, just in case. Kerry can't sit still.

Ball one.

Tony watches on the monitor from the clubhouse. His fellow maintenance staff members are placing pre-emptive plastic champagne-proof covering over furniture and fixtures, but Tony can't take his eyes off the screen.

Ball two.

Stan Greenwald is in the press box, pen and pad in hand, not writing. He watches intently as Will swings, and misses.

Strike one.

The crowd emits a thunderous moan. Ted Beasley is watching through binoculars from his owner's box. Phil Taylor and Al are in the dugout, trying to look calm for the sake of the team. Al's leg shakes uncontrollably as he flashes the sign and Will nods. An angry fan with a banner that reads simply "FRAUD" boos loudly. The pitcher winds and delivers.

CRACK!

The crowd is stunned to silence for a second before its collective volume swells to a volcanic roar. The ball has been launched, ripped very high and very far, into deep left. It soars over the fence into a sea of skyward-reaching humanity.

Foul.

The crowd is on the verge of a mass psychotic episode. The count is 2-2. The pitcher winds and throws a ninety-seven-mile-per-hour fastball. It's not going where he wanted it to go. It's coming in high, and inside. Will catches the ball's path, brings in his elbows and instinctively leans back. Kerry gasps.

Another sharp crack silences the crowd like a massive speaker blowing, so abruptly, the stadium hums and reverberates an eerie aftermath of interrupted mania.

Somehow, the ball has not hit Will, but the opposite. Off the sound of contact, the center fielder turns and gives chase, as the ball arcs high into the air toward deep center. Will stands in the batter's box, staring, unable to move. Andrew and Stephanie Dobbs are standing as well, not conscious of how they got that way. The players and coaches from both teams start slowly walking out of the dugouts for a better view, staring like zombies mesmerized by the path of the small round object flying through the air high above the Bronx. Tony, and now all of the clubhouse staff, are glued to the broadcast monitor in the clubhouse. Ted Beasley puts down his binoculars and leans forward, staring though the glass. Stan drops his pen and stares wide-eyed at the ball's flight. Kerry has sunken into her seat, afraid to move, as if doing so may somehow affect the trajectory of the ball. She's not sure what she wants to happen. Millions of people are all watching and wondering the same thing.

Where will it land?

The center fielder continues to track his target over his shoulder, running headlong toward the wall. The ball continues its flight into deep center field. As it begins its downward path toward earth, he looks to check the distance to the wall. As he, and the ball reach it, he leaps.

At its apex, the center fielder's gloved hand rises to the top edge of the wall, and as it does, the ball lands in it. He glances off the wall and lands safely on the warning track with the ball securely nestled in the webbing of his glove.

Kerry and Will's parents gasp. The crowd is silent. They don't feel compelled to cheer, or boo, the winning team similarly unsure and frozen. Normally, a celebration would erupt at this point, but normally, the world does not witness a baseball player launch a ball to the one place where his possible superpowers would continue to be a mystery.

"You gotta be friggin' kidding me," Stan says, still staring.

The center fielder is staring at the ball in his glove as if to make sure that what just happened really just happened. Will is staring blankly into center field. The center fielder starts jogging in, straight towards Will. A moment later he reaches him, and hands him the ball.

"I believe this belongs to you," he says. "Thought you might want to have it."

Will holds it for a moment. "Why?" he says as he hands it back. "You just won the World Series."

The center fielder stands there for a long moment with a strange look on his face, the ball in his hand. He looks at Will, who is smiling.

"Congratulations," Will says. The two players just stare at each other, as millions watch.

"WOOOOOOOOHOOOOOOO!!!!!" The center fielder lets out a huge victory cry as he throws his glove in the air and breaks the incredibly awkward silence. His teammates rush out of the dugout to shout and hug and celebrate in classic World Series winning fashion. Will fades away, toward the Yankees dugout, almost unnoticed amongst the wild infield celebration.

The overwhelmingly Yankee crowd doesn't know exactly how to react to such a historic loss. Some fans are crying, some are cheering. Some don't know how to feel. Overall, there is a sense that even though their team lost, the game they love took a beating, fought back, and won. Tony looks at the monitor, shaking his head and smiling. Kerry and Will's parents are hugging and smiling. Stan Greenwald has retrieved his pen and is writing furiously in his pad, the story he's been working on now practically writing itself. Ted Beasley stands, staring, his mouth opens to say something, but he doesn't know what to say or who to say it to. Phil Taylor looks over at Al Gianfranca, and does a double take.

"Are you crying?" Phil asks.

"Yes, I'm friggin' crying!" Al blubbers.

"Why?" asks Phil.

"I have no friggin' idea!" he sobs. Phil rubs Al's head and laughs.

Before descending into the dugout, Will spots Kerry in the crowd and whispers, "I did it." She whispers back, "I love you."

Three hours later, after the press conferences and celebrations and champagne-soaked interviews from the visitor's clubhouse have ended, there is still plastic covering everything in the Yankee clubhouse in anticipation of the celebration that was not to be. Will is the last one there. He's slowly packing up his locker.

"You still here?" Tony asks.

"Oh, hey, Tony," Will says turning to see his friend. "I'll be out of here in a minute."

"No, take your time," he says, leaning on his broom. "It's all kind of hard to believe, isn't it?"

"What part?" Will says, smiling.

"Just, you know, all of it."

"It's… yeah, it's a lot." Will goes back to packing. Tony notices a sadness in him.

"You all right?" he asks.

"Yeah, it's just. Man. In the last two years I almost died, acquired… superpowers or something, had a son, won the World Series and lost the World Series."

"A lot of curveballs," Tony says.

"Yeah. I was a batting superhero, and now I just feel like I'm just trying to make contact, you know?" Will says. "Stay in the game. I have to. I have to. I just wanted to play baseball, and find my dad. That's it. I didn't want anything else, you know?" Tony leans the broom against a wall and takes a seat next to Will.

"No luck yet?" Tony asks.

"No. Guess I'm just waiting. I'll keep waiting. Waiting and playing. That's all I can do."

Tony takes a deep breath and looks straight ahead. "Will, anyone can hit the straight ball, ya know, but you can measure a man by how he handles the curve. You try to do the right thing as the world is chucking curveballs at you, left right, up, and down. You might not always be able to hit a homer, or even make contact… and you get beaned. Hard. It hurts."

As Tony is talking, Will is taken aback as he sees tears forming in his eyes.

"But knowing what the right thing to do is, and trying to do that, is what being a man is about. You get hit, you get back up, you keep going. You keep playing. You don't quit. No matter how much it hurts. You keep fighting. You are a good man, Will Dobbs," he says, still staring straight ahead, tears now rolling down his cheeks. "Not all of us are."

"Tony?" Will asks, concerned.

"You can't always do the right thing," Tony continues, "Sometimes you fail, sometimes it's the hardest thing you'll ever do, but you gotta try, you always gotta try. And I tried, son, I swear I did. I tried."

Will recoils at Tony's words as their meaning takes hold.

"No," he says in disbelief. "Tony Ross? You're Carlton Rossi?"

Tony nods.

"I applied for the job as soon as I heard you got drafted," Tony says. "I had read your story in the papers and I knew it had to be you. I watched you grow up, son. I had to see you with my own eyes. I wasn't ever gonna tell you. I figured you hate me. I just wanted to see you play. I wasn't gonna tell you. But Stan found out."

"Stan Greenwald?" Will asks.

"Yeah. He dug around and found my records in Boston. He wants to write an article. He said I should tell you first. I'm sorry. I'll quit, Will. I'm sor—"

Will interrupts him with a huge hug he's needed for twenty-four years. Tony wipes back tears from his eyes.

"I tried, son. I'm sorry."

"It's OK, Dad. It's OK. I don't hate you. Don't cry. I am so glad we found each other. It's all OK now. I never hated you. I hated not being able to find you."

Tony looks his son in the eye. "Thank you," he says. "Thanks for finding me."

Will hugs him again. Tony holds his son tight and breathes deeply. He is relieved and overjoyed. Will is as well. Of course, there are questions, and anger to be dealt with at the right time, which is not now. Will stays still with his dad in his arms, savoring the feeling of a finally whole heart.

CHAPTER 31

Will, Tony and Stan have a long chat over pizza in Stan's office that culminates in Stan's final article: "Making Contact: America's Pastime, and the Power of a Father's Love."

Will's understanding of Tony's reluctance to come forward helps alleviate Tony's initial anger toward Stan for forcing the issue. In the article, Stan steers clear of his speculations of Will's **PED** usage and possible deceptions, and writes of his motivation behind it all, love. He writes of Tony's physical and emotional pain after the car accident and loss of his wife, and how it all was too much for him to handle. How he soon started drinking again, and feeling like he had no option, did the unthinkable. He left his baby boy on the steps of the local **NYPD** station, changed his name, and got on a bus to Buffalo. He continued drowning his sorrows for many years, until the day he happened upon an article about a promising young high school ball player named William, adopted by a couple in Boston, with dreams of playing for the New York Yankees.

Stan writes about his part in bringing this father and son together again after discovering an obscure employment document that recorded an alias for an unassuming Yankee clubhouse janitor, Tony Ross.

He writes about magic, hope, striving for things unobtainable and believing in things unexplainable. He writes of the inadvertent irreparable damage Will has done to America's favorite game, and the toll it has taken on the fans, and himself personally. He also writes that whatever brought on Will's abilities and whether their continued existence is real or not, people around the world got to witness something special, something miraculous, something that made them feel things they have never felt before, and most likely never will again.

The article concludes with the announcement that Stan is retiring from his career with the New York Post, and Will Dobbs is retiring from baseball.

EPILOGUE

Three years after his retirement, Will is thoroughly enjoying the life of a mere mortal. He coaches the local little league team, and still does the occasional charity appearance, minus the superhuman hitting displays. Will Jr. watches the games and events, not quite old enough to participate. Will and Kerry have formed their own organization dedicated to connecting adopted kids with their birth parents. Malcolm Pruitt is CEO and lead investigator, and Stan Greenwald writes all the promotional material and helps with the investigations. Will is constantly courted for motivational speeches, coaching jobs in the majors and minors, and broadcast announcing jobs. He'll get back into the spotlight, and start making money again, but there's plenty for the time being, so he's just enjoying spending time with his father, and being the best one he can be for Will Jr. He's also preparing for another fatherly adventure, with a baby girl due in six months.

Tony worked for the Yankees for another few months after Will's final game. He felt bad about leaving the dream job that the team had been so kind in giving him, but eventually, everyone agreed that Tony deserved an early retirement. He reluctantly agreed, only when Will bought lifetime season tickets, so he could go to the games whenever he wanted.

The Dobbs family is outside in the back yard celebrating Independence Day. Will's parents, Kerry's parents, Will Jr. and Tony are there. Kerry baked a cake and when Will Jr. cried upon learning it was not his birthday, candles were quickly located and utilized and the Independence Day/fourth-and-a-half birthday celebration commenced.

"Good boy!" Kerry says, as Will Jr. blows out the candles. "OK, come on, let's go inside and eat this before the skeeters come out!"

"But I want to play catch with the glove Grandpa Tony got me!"

Kerry gives him a look. Then she looks at Tony, who shrugs and smiles.

"It's getting dark, and Nana and Pop Pop have to get going," she says sternly. "Five minutes."

"Yay!" says Will Jr. grabbing the glove from the table. "Come on, Dad!"

"I'm coming, I'm coming," Will says. He hunts around the grass for a ball until he finds one. "OK, I got the ball. Here we go."

"Five minutes," she says to Will.

"Got it, we'll be back in five."

"I'll bring the cake in," offers Tony.

"You just want the first bite!" Kerry says, laughing.

"You bet your bottom dollar I do," says Tony.

Kerry's parents head inside as well. Will and Will Jr. find a nice clear area deep in the back yard some distance from the house. Will takes Will Jr.'s small hands and shows him how to put his glove on.

"OK, so you put your glove on this hand, like this," Will says to his son. "Make sure all of your fingers are in there. They in there?"

"Yes," Will Jr. says.

"How many? Four? Six?"

"Dada! Five!"

"Oh yeah, that's right. OK good. Now squeeze." Will Jr. grimaces and squeezes. "Good. Don't worry, it will get softer the more you play. OK, I'm going to squat down like a catcher over there. You're the pitcher, you stand right here and try to throw it all the way to Daddy, OK?"

"OK."

Will hands the ball to his son, walks about thirty feet away, turns and squats, catcher style. He talks in exaggerated baseball announcer voice.

"AND NOW…on the mound for the New York Yankees… straight out of Five Corners Preschool, Mrs. Greenbaum's 4s class…William Dobbs, Jr.!!!"

Will Jr. giggles at his dad's antics. "Daddy, stop it!" he says, laughing.

"OK. Show me what you got." Will slaps his hand and puts it out as a target. "Right here, big guy."

"OK."

Will Jr. sets. His dad smiles as he sees his son imitating the big-league players' stance and motions he's seen on TV. The regulation baseball looks huge in his tiny hand. He takes a step forward, and throws.

The force of the ball causes Will to yelp in surprise and pain as it hits his bare hands, and knocks him back, off his feet. Will gets up, shakes the sting out of his hands, and dusts himself off. Will Jr. is smiling. His father is staring at him, perplexed. We see a hint of a familiar red glimmer in Will Jr.'s eye. As Will stares, his son realizes that maybe he shouldn't be smiling.

"Sorry, Dada," he says.

Will looks at his son, then looks around, picks up a nearby two-by-four, and tosses the ball back to Will Jr. He gets into batting position, using the two-by-four as a makeshift bat.

"Do that again," he says.

Will Jr. gets set, rears back and throws another screaming bullet in his father's direction. Will connects with an all too familiar "CRACK!"

The ball flies and flies, and even though there is nothing blocking the view, it soon is invisible due to sheer distance. Will Jr.'s jaw drops in amazement. Will drops the two-by-four.

"Don't tell Mommy," he says.

THE END